Spencer

Hathaway House, Book 19

Dale Mayer

SPENCER: HATHAWAY HOUSE, BOOK 19
Beverly Dale Mayer
Valley Publishing Ltd.

Copyright © 2023 Beverly Dale Mayer

All rights reserved. Except for use in any review, the reproduction or utilization of this work in whole or in part by any electronic, mechanical or other means, now known or hereafter invented, including xerography, photocopying and recording, or in any information storage or retrieval system, is forbidden without the written permission of the publisher.

This is a work of fiction. Names, characters, places, brands, media, and incidents are either the product of the author's imagination or are used fictitiously. Any resemblance to actual events, locales, or persons, living or dead, is entirely coincidental.

ISBN-13: 978-1-773367-77-4
Print Edition

Books in This Series

Aaron, Book 1

Brock, Book 2

Cole, Book 3

Denton, Book 4

Elliot, Book 5

Finn, Book 6

Gregory, Book 7

Heath, Book 8

Iain, Book 9

Jaden, Book 10

Keith, Book 11

Lance, Book 12

Melissa, Book 13

Nash, Book 14

Owen, Book 15

Percy, Book 16

Quinton, Book 17

Ryatt, Book 18

Spencer, Book 19

Timothy, Book 20

Hathaway House, Books 1–3

Hathaway House, Books 4–6

Hathaway House, Books 7–9

About This Book

Welcome to Hathaway House. Rehab Center. Safe Haven. Second chance at life and love.

Getting into Hathaway House before his friend wasn't the plan, but that's how it worked out, leaving Spencer in a state of waiting for his buddy to arrive. In the meantime, he has work to do. Right from day one he wants to establish and to maintain some independence in this way-too-busy center, luckily meeting the groundskeeper on his first attempt at getting coffee.

Bella has been looking after the Hathaway House grounds for over five years. Although she's seen and interacted with many of the residents here, she never really got close to any—until Spencer. Now she can't help but watch his progress in awe, as he moves through his program with dedication. Is he trying so hard to show off to his soon-to-arrive friend? Or for her sake? Or because he's eager to leave the center and start his new improved future?

A future that won't be in Hathaway House and one that might not include her …

Prologue

SPENCER NEWCOMB SHARED a semiprivate VA hospital room with his friend Timothy Watkins. "I don't get it," Spencer said. "Why are you trying to get into this place so much?"

"Because it's got a fantastic rep," Timothy murmured. "And this place sucks."

Well, Spencer wouldn't argue with that assessment of their current scenario because, well, it was true. There was an awful lot that they didn't like about it here.

Timothy added, "And you and I are a team. We've been through so much already, and we should stick together in healing as well."

"And what makes you think this Hathaway place will be any better?"

"How can it be worse?"

"It's still a long trip for nothing."

"Or it could be a long trip for everything," Timothy argued. "You know, in some of the online forums, the guys talk about the different methods the guys at Hathaway House have of getting people back on their feet. I'm willing to try." He frowned. "I think some of your friends went there too."

Spencer rolled his head toward Timothy and asked, "Yeah, who?"

"Percy, for one."

Spencer's eyebrows shot up at that.

Timothy continued. "Ha, and didn't you know Lance?"

"Well, I know *a* Lance," Spencer replied. "Doesn't mean I know the one who you're talking about."

"No, that's true, but I think you'd probably do some good to ask them. Then fill me in, but I'm already sold. We both should sign up. You never know. You might get into this place before I do, knowing Percy and Lance."

"And maybe not," Spencer argued, with a smile. "After all, it's not as if I'll necessarily jump ahead in line. You know, if a place is this good, it'll have a queue waiting to get in."

"Yeah, it sure will," Timothy agreed. "I'm just filling out the application now, but you know how I hate all this paperwork and dredging up all my medical history. Why do they want us to list all this stuff on their stupid forms when they also want our medical reports? Such a waste to ask for things twice." Shaking his head, Timothy was typing on his phone. "I sent you the link. Maybe if you're dealing with this headache of paperwork too, I'll be happier dealing with my application."

Spencer's phone beeped, and he looked at the link on his screen, still undecided.

Timothy nodded at his buddy. "Try it. I mean, what's the harm?"

After Timothy headed off for his therapy session, Spencer looked again at the link and frowned. It sounded a little bit too good to be true. It had been a really long time since Spencer got taken in by a dream, but it did seem to him that, if there were any truth to the Hathaway hype, some of his friends who already did their rehab there might very well give him answers, one way or the other.

So Spencer sent off a couple emails and followed up with a couple text messages. When Lance got back to him and said, *If you get an opportunity, go,* Spencer was really surprised. Then he got an email back from Percy, saying, *Go, man, go.* After that, Spencer filled out the application without another thought. He told Timothy to get his butt in gear and finish his application too. Spencer's internal critic highly expected to not get in; a place like that would have a long waiting list.

Nobody was more surprised than him and even Timothy when, just two days later, Spencer got an email response from Hathaway House, asking for more medical records. Spencer quickly filled out everything that needed to be done and then sent it all off, nudging Timothy once more to get the lead out. "We're partners in this. I need my partner on this leg of the journey."

Timothy nodded, but Spencer didn't see his buddy jumping online.

When Spencer got a phone call not very long afterward, it was from the manager of the center. She introduced herself and said, "I'm calling about your wish to join Hathaway House."

"Well, I was … I had … I know both Percy and Lance," he muttered.

"They do give you glowing references," she noted quietly. "We do prefer to take people who understand just how different we are here," she murmured.

"I don't know how different you are, but I can tell you that, in all the other rehab places I've been, nobody's ever given me a good recommendation for any of them."

She laughed. "No, and it's not an easy road that you guys are on," she stated, "which is one of the reasons why we try hard to make your stay here as pleasant and as productive as possible. I do have an opening, but it will be in about six weeks. ... Wait. Let me check on that. Hang on a minute." She came back a few minutes later and said, "I have a cancellation. I could move you up to three weeks."

"Wow. Seriously?"

"Yes. You just tell me if you want to proceed and arrange for your departure accordingly, and then I need to contact your doctors. We have to start that whole transfer procedure. Your treating physicians must give their permission for you and your records to be moved. In which case the three-week opening could be too tight."

Spencer frowned at that. "I don't know if they'll go for it," he noted, "but I would like to try."

"Good enough," she said. "Leave it in my hands, and I'll get back to you, when I find out a date that we're good to go." And, with that, she hung up.

When Spencer just asked Timothy about the status of his application, he moaned. "Man, you know how I feel about filling out this application. I got started, and I didn't get any further."

"Right, but maybe you want to now," Spencer added, "since I already got in."

Timothy looked at him, stunned. "What? What do you mean?" he cried out in dismay. "I only told you about it a few days ago."

"She just called me," he said, motioning at the phone. "She'll get the process started. She had a cancellation, and I can get in three weeks from now. Apparently it'll take that long to get everything together."

In shock, his friend collapsed onto his bed beside Spencer's.

"Get your application in," Spencer urged. "You never know. We could go at the same time."

And that was finally enough for Timothy to jump on board. "I'd better," he snapped. "I can't believe you got in before me."

"You took too long," Spencer stated bluntly. "You can't talk about these places and their queues. You have to make a decision and jump."

"Since when did you ever jump?" he muttered.

"Hey, you might be surprised." Spencer laughed. "Sometimes I don't need to be persuaded. I can see a good thing in front of me."

"Says you," he protested. "I'm still in shock."

"Well, deal with it," Spencer murmured, "because I'm going. Anything to get out of here will be better than where we are."

"Exactly." Timothy looked up and asked, "If I don't get in right away, you'll let me know what it's like, right?"

"Absolutely." Spencer smiled at his friend. "And you may want to pass it around that there's another option too. We've got a lot of friends here who could use a chance to get out and to get something better."

"I know," he murmured. "I'll do that. I'll start drumming up some more interest in the Hathaway place—but not until I get my spot secured," he declared. "No way will anybody else jump that line on me."

At that, Spencer shook his head. "Then jump in again. You were too slow to fill out the application. I just did what you said."

"Wow, I won't be slow anymore," Timothy muttered. And right then and there he finished it and submitted the form. "Done now," he announced, "and hopefully I can get in too."

Chapter 1

For Spencer, that three weeks had turned into four, before the doctors were done with the transfer of the paperwork and everybody had signed off to their satisfaction. And joy of joys, Spencer's buddy Timothy had also been accepted. Apparently Hathaway House had an expanded wing and were taking in people off their waiting list. So Timothy was coming in a couple weeks behind Spencer. The fact that they would be there at the same time was huge. They'd been friends since forever. They'd even gotten injured at the same time, which was not what Spencer wanted his friend to deal with, but, considering the alternatives, still a good place to be so that they weren't alone when facing what was coming at them.

As soon as Spencer arrived, he sensed a completely different atmosphere to the place. But also a concerning one because, as he sat in the front reception waiting area to get checked in, he was surrounded by chaos. People coming and going. Almost too much by the time the receptionist got up, came around, and smiled at him.

"Hi," she greeted him.

He looked at her and shook his head. "Are you guys sure you're ready for me today?"

"Oh, we are. It's intake day, and it's a little bit on the crazy side, and technically you weren't expected for a few hours yet," she explained. "Apparently your trip went faster than anybody thought it would."

"Ah, well, as long as you're ready for me," he replied cautiously.

She smiled and nodded. "We are, indeed. This is Joseph." She pointed to a large orderly with a big smile on his face. "He'll take you to your room, and you can get out of that chair and rest a bit."

"Good." Spencer nodded. "Transportation in any way, shape, or form is just painful."

"Yep," she agreed, with a gentle smile, "we see it all the time, and we're sorry. The process is just a little scrambled today. You won't see this all the time here."

"Good," he answered, a little worried. He looked up to see Joseph still smiling at him.

With a wave of his arm, Joseph said, "Come on. Let's get you settled in." And he picked up Spencer's bag and moved the wheelchair down the hallway.

"I could probably push a little bit," Spencer offered, "if the bag is too much."

"Nope, isn't too much. I've slung a lot bigger bags in my time."

"So were you in the military?"

"I was a marine," he noted, with a proud smile. "Now I'm here."

"And you're happy here?" he asked.

"Yep. I came because some of my friends needed the help," he added, "and now I work here. And I wouldn't want to work anywhere else."

That was an endorsement Spencer hadn't expected to hear. "Wow, is it that good?"

"It is that good," he responded, "but it's not for me to

tell you. That you'll find out firsthand for yourself."

"I hope so," he muttered. "I wasn't doing very well at the last place."

"We hear that a lot too," Joseph noted calmly. "Don't lie to your team, don't cheat yourself here, dive in and do the best you can because it's your one shot for completely changing your life," he said. "You won't even know what I mean, not until you get down the rehab pathway in a few weeks, and then you can see how different things are."

"I hope so," Spencer admitted. "We've heard a lot about the place and the systems and the staff here, but people talk, and they don't have the same issues, or you're always afraid that it worked for them, but it won't work for you."

Joseph laughed. "And I totally agree with you. You shouldn't be listening to anybody else's take on this. You should be making your own assessments and figuring it out yourself."

They turned down a short hallway. "And, in order to do that, you must have an open mind, and as soon as you stop the initial judgments, you'll find all kinds of things filtering inside," Joseph added. "A lot of power is here, and I haven't figured out yet whether it's a positive healing collective mind-set that helps raise everybody's ability to do better or just that the techniques here are so different and so effective. I'm blessed to not have been part of the side that you're on," he shared, "but I certainly see the difference for the people who are patients here."

"And what about your friend?" Spencer asked curiously.

"Friends," Joseph corrected. "Several of them, and by now multiples more I've convinced to come here. And they're all doing just fine. We stay in touch. Sometimes they come back for a visit, sometimes just for the memories, because connections are made here. Connections that you want to keep because they mean something."

Joseph stopped outside a door. "We just recently started a huge reunion every year, and it's been good to see people. Here they get a chance to learn some new techniques that could apply to their situations or improvements that they can do that nobody knew about back when they were here."

He put down Spencer's bag and opened the door, propping it open. "This place is always growing, always changing, because of the people involved, whether patients or staff. So again don't shortchange yourself, fully explore everything offered here, and I think you'll be wonderfully surprised."

Inside Spencer's room, Joseph helped him out of the wheelchair, as if understanding how stiff and sore Spencer was from the trip, and then onto the bed, where he collapsed on his back, shudders of relief racking through his system.

"Now," Joseph said, "I'm not a nurse, but I can get one, and we can do something for the pain, if needed."

"No." Spencer shook his head. "It's not pain from the injuries. It's from being in the same position without moving for so long."

"I get it." Joseph nodded. "Whatever it is you need, just ask, no explanations necessary."

"I'm glad to hear that." Spencer sighed. "My recovery is still pretty rough."

"It is, indeed, and that's all right," he stated. "I know that Dani will be here soon. However, in the meantime, do you want water, a cup of coffee, or something else I can get for you?"

He stared at Joseph in surprise. "Both of those would be lovely."

Joseph smiled. "How do you take your coffee?"

"Black," he murmured. "And, if the water's got no ice, that would be even better."

And, with that, Joseph disappeared.

Already seeing a change in Hathaway House's atmosphere, Spencer felt as if he were at a first-class restaurant or a five-star hotel. As he looked around at the fairly sparse but comfortable room with the huge windows, he noted the rolling hills and horses and white picket fences outside. He stared in surprise. "Horses," he murmured to himself. "Good Lord."

Somebody rode a lawnmower along the inside edge of a fence, and somebody else trimmed rhododendrons and other plants he didn't recognize. A team of three or four gardeners currently handled the landscape, but this place was huge, so lawn maintenance would probably be a full-time job.

Spencer eased back into bed again, taking a deep breath, trying to unlock some of the muscles in his back and his hips. He took several deep breaths again, trying not to force his diaphragm to his belly and then cramp his bladder, which was already protesting. He should have made the trip to the bathroom on the way to his bed.

Breathing gently to expand his chest and to open up his lungs—another area where the injuries and scar tissue seemed to be never-ending—he wouldn't wait any longer, and he slid his feet to the floor and slowly stood. His prosthetic needed to come off soon; otherwise his stump would be sore too. He'd been vain enough to travel with it, but he shouldn't have. He only had a couple inches of thigh bone, and, of course, that leg was stiff after this trip here. However, if he moved carefully, he should get to his en suite bathroom and back on his own two legs.

By the time he returned to his bed, he was covered in

sweat. He managed to sit down again, and he lowered his pants, wishing the door was closed, but it wasn't, and he didn't care enough to make that trip. With a great big sigh, he removed his prosthetic. Seeing the raw angry stump, he whistled. "That was a stupid decision," he murmured.

"*A* decision," a woman noted, studying the stump in front of him.

He flushed and pulled his pants up again. "Sorry. I just couldn't stand to have it on any longer."

"You probably shouldn't have had it on this long," she murmured, looking at him. She stepped forward and held out a hand. "I'm Dani."

He stared at her in surprise. She was way younger, way prettier, and looked more like a model than somebody who ran a rehab center. He shook her hand. "Thank you for letting me in."

She grinned. "You are most welcome, but we'll have to take care of that." She pointed at his leg.

"I know. I'm just not sure what the answer is."

"That's not my department either," she replied, "but I can guarantee you that you'll do an awful lot better here in a few weeks, once that's calmed down."

He nodded. "I don't know whether it's just the inevitability of an amputation or my prosthetic doesn't fit correctly or what," he shared. "Yet, every time I use it, I get into trouble."

"So it could be a number of things," she agreed, with a smile. "We will address it later. However, it's not an issue right now because your team will probably prefer to have you in a wheelchair first, then graduate to crutches, letting that stump heal properly."

She handed him an iPad. "This is your scheduler. It's

how you keep track of what's going on in your world here. Plus you can open up your emails, check what's on the menu, et cetera, all on that."

He looked at it in surprise. "Seriously?"

She nodded and clicked a few buttons. "Here's your schedule. This is your team."

After that, he almost drowned in data, so much information flew at him.

Finally she stopped. "And I know that was a ton of stuff to hit you with all at once. So just peck away at it, figure it out, and, if you have any questions, get back to me." She pointed out her phone number already keyed in for him, under his team. "Your remote also has my contact number displayed."

She took a couple steps closer. "We do have release forms and all that good stuff here." She handed him a clipboard and went over them. By the time he'd signed away his life, he was a bit dazed.

She smiled. "Now you'll get a couple days to just rest and recuperate from the trip, and then we'll start the testing stage. Some of the tests we'll start with tomorrow or the next day," she noted, "depending on how bad things are, and then we'll get you into your rehab program and see about getting you back on track immediately."

"That sounds good," Spencer noted.

And, with that, she disappeared.

Not very long afterward, Joseph returned, carrying a large cup of water and a coffee for Spencer. "Here you go." He rolled the small table nearer to his hospital bed. "I don't know whether Dani's been here or not, but dinner's at five. If you can't make it, you let one of us know." Joseph said, pointing at the buttons and alarms on the remote. "Somebody will come grab dinner for you."

"Thanks." Spencer nodded. "Right now I'm a bit overwhelmed and just need to close my eyes."

"Makes sense to me. Don't you worry about it. You rest, and, when you feel better, we'll all be around, waiting to help you out." With that, Joseph was gone too.

BELLA CAMDEN LIFTED her shovel, wiped the sweat off her face, and surveyed the garden bed that she had just completed. It was looking good. Now if only she could keep Helga, the rambunctious Newfoundlander from rolling in the fresh dirt. Not that she'd mind if she did. The animals here added another layer to her work but also to her sense of well-being. She often had lunch on the fence, while visiting with the horses and, of course, the little llama. That Dani couldn't keep herself from helping animals—make that people too—in need just made her an even better boss to work with. Nothing made her happier than to be outside on such a beautiful day as today. She preferred to start very early if she could and get done by noon or at least by 1:00 p.m., but today they had a lot of transplanting work, so they were running behind. Still, it was what it was, and she was good with that.

"Hey, Bella," Charlie called out. "I think I'm done."

"You and me both," she said on a groan. "And not a moment too soon either, considering the heat rolling in."

"Right," he agreed. "Back tomorrow morning at six?"

"Yep, six a.m. every day this week." Of course that was her team's hours. Bella began work at 5:00 a.m.

She ran a team of three gardeners here at the center. And

then she brought in extra help as needed. Hathaway House was a busy place, and just maintaining the driveways and the flower beds was time consuming. The garden paths required a lot of attention to accommodate people who weren't fully mobile. So Bella looked specifically for problems, where bigger rocks were showing up or some paths needed another layer of gravel or some needed packing rolled atop them. She took pride in the work she did here. She'd been here for four years and had gotten to know a ton of people, both patients and staff alike, and Bella was delighted to do her part to help anyone get outside more.

She had her own apartment on the grounds as well because she was full-time, but she was the only one of the landscaping team who did. And still it made her smile in delight every time she got up in the morning. She usually was in the pool by 4:30 a.m. and then started her day. And, when she took her first break, she grabbed breakfast. Often she didn't take a break; she just worked right through, until she could get through her chosen projects for the day.

Then she would quit and go in and eat. Dennis often left her food in the fridge, knowing that she'd come and go at odd hours. She seemed to be the only one who did, although she met Chef Ilse more than a few times herself because, as the head chef here, Ilse came in early as well.

Bella loaded up her little trailer with all the equipment and hopped on to the attached small lawn tractor that she used to drag the tools around this place and headed back to the huge shed, where she stored everything. She was always the last one to leave and always locked up. They couldn't afford to lose any equipment, and, so far, there'd been no thefts or vandalism. Now she was hot and sweaty, and that pool was looking mighty fine.

Helga woofed at her, startling her. She laughed and walked over to the big three-legged baby. She crouched in front of her and got headbutted for her efforts. She chuckled and scrubbed Helga's thick neck, then up to her ears. "You're right. I've been busy all day, haven't I? Too busy to give you the attention you deserve."

Helga woofed in agreement and nudged her again.

Laughing, Bella obliged before finally standing up and giving her a big hug. "That's it for now. I need a shower. Then to eat." With one last pat on Helga's head, Bella headed home.

Back at her place, she had a quick shower. Her stomach grumbled. She'd started early, as usual, and once again she hadn't eaten. So right now she needed food more than she needed a swim. She threw on a simple sundress and headed up to the dining room. She was a little bit late for lunch but hoped she had enough time left to see a selection of fresh food.

Chapter 2

AS BELLA WALKED up to the buffet line in the dining room, Dennis came around the counter. "Hey, I didn't see you earlier."

"No," she replied, "we worked late today and still didn't quite get it all done either."

"Ah, let's not focus on that. Instead let's get you some grub, and then you can relax."

"Thanks, I missed the designated lunch hours again."

He shook his head. "You know how I feel about that."

She smiled. "I do know how you feel about that. You're one of the few people who are adamant about everybody getting fed on time."

"It's not about *on time*," he corrected her. "It's making sure that you feed your body, while you demand it to do all this other work."

She winced. "I stand corrected."

"What would you like?" Dennis asked. "We still have some leftovers here."

When she saw the fish sautéed in butter, she immediately pointed it out. "You do fish so well here, and I never even used to eat it."

"*Tsk, tsk,*" he muttered, with a smile. "Come on. Let's get you a plateful."

By the time she had that and a huge salad and some

steamed veggies, she was good. She took it all outside, where she sat down on the deck. As she watched somebody she hadn't seen before, a man in a wheelchair at the entrance to the deck, she smiled at him. "Hey. Are you eating out here?"

He winced. "Honestly I have no idea. I think I'm lost."

"Did you eat?"

He shook his head. "No, I didn't, and that's probably part of the reason. I followed the scent of food, but I might have missed the lunch hour. I just arrived today."

At that, Dennis walked over. "I heard you are a new arrival. You must be Spencer. And I'm Dennis." He reached over and shook Spencer's hand. "What can I get you?"

"I don't want to be a bother," he replied hurriedly. "I didn't realize that I had slept so long."

"You'll find, in the first couple days, that you'll do a lot of napping." Dennis smiled. "Most patients expect to be in better shape when they arrive, but, the fact of the matter is, it takes time to adjust."

"If you say so." Spencer looked over at her plate. "Her selection looks great," he noted, "but maybe a bit of carbs to go with it."

"Absolutely on the carbs," Dennis agreed. "Just sit here with her, and I'll see what I can do." And, with that, Dennis disappeared.

Spencer looked at her and hesitated.

She smiled. "Please join me." She motioned at her table. "I work here. I'm one of the people who keep the grounds out there beautiful," she added. "And I was late myself, so I missed lunch too."

He smiled. "Probably not a good thing to do around this place," he stated, looking at her plate. "That's quite a nice selection of food."

"And one thing you'll learn very quickly here," she shared. "Not only is the selection nice but it's good fresh food, and the cooking comes from heart, which always seems to make a difference."

He looked at her in surprise and then nodded. "You're right. A lot of food that my grandmother made I never particularly liked, but, because she made it, it always tasted so much better than the same stuff that my buddies' mothers would make," he said. "I never told them that of course."

"Sometimes that happens." She chuckled. "Dennis and the kitchen staff are wonderful. You'll have to meet Ilse. She's the chef in the back. I see her more often than anybody just because I'm up and in here early in the morning. They run a wonderful place here," she added. "You'll do just fine."

"Thank you." Spencer nodded. "I came because of the recommendation of several friends, so I'm hoping that you're correct. I'm hoping everybody's correct. It's hard to know what to do sometimes. You give up on having any options, and then suddenly there's one, and it makes you nervous to even follow through because you don't know if you can believe what people say."

"I get that," she agreed, with a smile. "I think that's life. We hear so much stuff, and you never know how to filter out the good from the bad and what's even realistic versus somebody's overenthusiastic pipe dream."

He chuckled. "I was thinking the same thing." He pulled his wheelchair closer to the table. "Do you mind?" he asked hesitantly. "I don't want to disturb your meal."

"Absolutely. I don't mind. This space is for everybody here. I'm Bella Camden, by the way."

"Spencer Newcomb." He smiled. "I could take another table, if you wanted to be alone."

"I'm good," she said. "As soon as I'm done eating, I'll go for a swim."

He stared at her. "A swim?"

She chuckled. "If you look over the railing, there is a pool *and* a hot tub."

At the sound of that, his face lit up. "Now that would get me going a lot faster than a lot of things. I saw the horses"—he pointed to the fenced-in area in the distance and the beautiful black horse that was the closest—"and I haven't been on a horse in a very long time. I never thought I might get back to riding again," he shared, "so I was surprised to see them here." He stared, a look of rapture on his face, before his shoulders slumped, and a heavy sigh slipped out.

"That's one of Dani's projects," Bella stated immediately wondering at the thoughts running through his mind. "Those are her babies, and I think some of them are used for riding sessions with some of the patients. So, if it interests you, let them know. I think they're open to doing whatever works for you."

"And that ... would be amazing in itself."

Such hope filled his gaze that she couldn't help but add, "I get it. My brother was here years ago, and I came to visit him one day, and I never left. See the little llama out there with the horses? She's a sweetheart too." She laughed and gave him a one-arm shrug. "At the time they needed somebody to do the gardens, and I'm an arborist, so this was right up my alley. Trying to keep this place as lush and as happy as possible for a lot of people appealed to me. So I just moved on in. Now that my brother's doing well on his own, it's all good."

"Wow, I heard something similar from Joseph."

"Joseph's a crackerjack." She grinned and gave him a

knowing look. "He's got a heart of gold too. Almost everybody here does. You can't do this job without that."

He nodded. "It certainly helps to have that personality. Sometimes when we're at the VA centers, it seems to be just a job to people, and even the staff don't appear to want to be there either. That makes it so that none of us want to be there, especially those of us who have no choice."

"Yep, I heard the same thing from my brother. But you're here now"—she nodded, with another big grin—"and you have no idea how your life is about to change."

At that, Dennis walked back out on the deck with a huge platter.

"Wow. I am hungry, but I'm not sure I can eat all this."

"One thing around here is, we won't starve you, but we don't like to waste food either," Dennis shared. "So, at each meal, assess your appetite, so you'll know more for next time. Plus I'll see how you do, so I can assess your appetite for next time too," he explained, with that contagious big Hathaway House smile. "Other than that, you eat up and enjoy."

SPENCER TUCKED INTO the food. Hot. Fresh. Tasty. He stopped several times to assess the amount of food on his plate, shook his head, and dug in some more. Good food, great company, and unbelievable surroundings. So far, it had been a strange but amazing arrival.

"Not sure what the reassessment is every time," Bella admitted, "but just watching you eat is fun."

He looked at her in surprise. "Honestly I'm startled because it's full of flavors. You get used to a place always pushing through a lot of people, and the food tastes as if it were pushed through too. It's usually bland because they're going for the lowest denominator in the taste of the food," he stated. "And it ends up having zero flavor. But this stuff? Wow, this is good."

"I'm sure you'll break some hearts here telling them that. Everybody at Hathaway House works hard to keep the patients happy," she declared. "So you'll be easy to please."

"I'll be easy to please as long as I see some progress," he replied, with an unhappy sigh. "I want other people's stories to be true, but I'm worried that their recommendations are not even close to being possible for me, and that I give up on it."

"In that case," she suggested, "reserve the judgment and do the best you can to just see how it goes initially. … Absolutely nothing here says that this has to be an all-or-nothing proposition. The Hathaway process is very much about finding what works for you. And then, if you ever want to get out and to get away for a bit, just let me know." She pointed to the grounds. "I can wheel you to the gardens, where you can sit and commune with Mother Nature for a while, just to get away from everything inside."

She continued. "The rehab program demands everything from you—hard work that leads to success. Yet it's not always easy being surrounded by all these people here because a lot of patients will have progress that you might think you should have. However, you can't compare yourself to everyone else. First off, they've been here longer than you have. And second? They aren't you. Your body isn't theirs," she stated quietly.

"And, on the flip side, everybody needs a timeout at some point. You can't always push yourself without your body paying the price." And, with that, she stood. "I'm heading home for a bit." She waved at him and added, "Take it easy and adjust. It'll all be good." And, with that, she was gone.

He finished off his plate, just as she was leaving, wondering what he should do with his empty dish. By then Dennis was already there.

He asked, "How was that for your tastes?"

"Excellent," he declared. "Much more flavorful than I expected."

"I know. If you came from a government facility," Dennis replied, "they tend to do everything without spices because you can't cater to everyone's special diets all at the same time." Dennis nodded. "Sometimes we do have people on special diets here, but instead we choose to give them the special diet and not make everybody pay."

Spencer laughed. "I like that. So far, I have to admit you guys have made it very easy to be here."

"Oh, that'll change once you get into your rehab program." Dennis chuckled. "Don't you worry. You'll work for it."

"That's fine. I'm not scared of work," he stated calmly. "I'm just hoping that the work won't be for naught.'

"It won't be," Dennis declared. "I've seen it happen time and time again. Sure there are cases where people don't show as much progress as they think they should, and they get depressed, and they can get angry. Then, all of a sudden, they see more progress than they thought even possible. They're surprised and shocked and absolutely delighted. You might find no progress, or you might find a ton of progress, followed by a little progress." Dennis shrugged. "Everybody's different. It's a matter of just being okay with the difference and letting yourself learn to do what you need to do to heal."

After those words of wisdom, Spencer couldn't say a whole lot, except to thank Dennis for the excellent meal.

As he pushed away from the table, Dennis asked, "Will you be okay with that until dinnertime?"

"Yes, I should be fine. I'm pretty sore from the trip here," he shared. "Yet when I left my room, I could smell the food. ... That was enough for me."

Dennis laughed. "And lunch was a while ago," he noted, "so the aromas weren't all that strong by the time you got here."

"Enough to lead me, like the Pied Piper and the rats," he joked. "I won't miss too many meals, not if this is a sample of what's to come."

"It's a sample," Dennis confirmed, with a bright smile. "Do you want to take a coffee or a bottle of water or some dessert back with you?"

He looked at him in surprise. "We can take food to our rooms?"

"Sure can," he replied. "You can have a meal in your room too, if you need to. And, if it ever comes to a point in time where you're just not capable of getting down here," he added, "you give me a buzz, and I will make sure I get a meal delivered to you. Nobody goes hungry in Hathaway House."

And such horror filled Dennis's voice at that concept that Spencer had to laugh. "Good to know. I think I'll be fine though today. I ate so much that I'm scared I'll be up all night."

"Oh, that's not fun either," Dennis noted. "Just so you know that you're welcome here anytime. We may have put away the hot food, but we always have sandwiches and salads and yogurt and the like in the coolers next to the coffee station." And, with that, he collected the dishes and disappeared into the kitchen.

Spencer rolled his wheelchair slowly past a big coffee setup and a glass-fronted fridge full of food, sandwiches, and even drinks—milk and juices. He studied the contents for a long moment and then grabbed a bottle of water and slowly made his way back to his room.

He had a lot to learn, but one of the things he already understood was that his body was the boss, and right now he'd already put in enough time sitting upright. To do anything else would probably cause him trouble. As he slowly returned to his room, he glanced outside. The sun was high in the far horizon. Spencer needed to tell Timothy that he was here. As soon as he got in bed, he texted his buddy.

You need to get here and fast. If nothing else, just for the food.

And then he shut off his phone and crashed. Again.

Chapter 3

BELLA WOKE EARLY the next morning, her mind immediately returning to the man she had met yesterday. "Spencer. Nice name," she muttered to herself. He was also an interesting character. He seemed to be in terrible pain yesterday, but still he'd made the effort to get up and to get some food and to look after himself. She had to appreciate that dedication and perseverance, when he had been already pushed to the wall, and yet he still found something to get him up and to keep him going.

A lot of people were here, and some were doing better than others. However, a few just seemed to never quite get it. But most of the time she was amazed at the resilience and the ethics that people put into their own care and healing. And they needed to because she was a huge advocate for looking after yourself, rather than trusting that the world would always be there to provide for you.

When it came to Hathaway House, however, the staff were advocates of the ultimate individualized in-patient care needed for each and every person. It blew her away how every patient's story was just so different. Yet the staff all rose to the challenge each and every time.

For Bella, she just handled gardens and pathways and all the landscape-related things that went into keeping this place running, even for those with disabilities. She knew nobody really understood what she did or what the needs for these patients entailed, especially if people had never been on crutches or in a wheelchair. How could they understand her job?

Plus, if you didn't have any experience with gardens, then you weren't aware of the miles and miles of pathways here—just what was involved to ensure their healthy growth and for their intrinsic beauty, plus knowledge that things could be dangerous for people if the grounds weren't properly maintained. But, for Bella, this was a huge responsibility, and she took it seriously.

By the time she'd worked three hours this morning, starting before sunrise, she was royally sweating already. She stopped, had a bottle of water, and noted her stomach was growling. She scooped up Hoppers and loaded him on her cart to return to his pen. She often took him out with her when she was doing work that allowed her to keep an eye on him. "I need food, Hoppers," she said, as she placed him into his fenced area. "I haven't been grazing all morning, like you have been."

His ears twitched, and he immediately stretched full out on his side, his nose twitching happily. With a chuckle, she headed up to the dining room, deliberately going through the patient hallways, looking to see if she could find out where Spencer was. But she found no sign of him.

As she walked into the dining area, she noted it was empty. She smiled at Dennis and waved. "I'm a little earlier today."

"Great," he greeted her. "Anything that spreads out the mealtime traffic is a good thing. How did you make out so far this morning?"

"Fine," she replied. "I'm working on the pathways at the

back pastures. It always amazes me how far some of these patients can travel by the time they're ready to leave here."

"And they can visit with loved ones and go down there often," he added. "It's also a very popular picnic spot."

"I had heard that. Saw a couple people there occasionally," she noted, "and I was wondering about whether we should put in some picnic tables, so people can just sit and enjoy the animals."

"You mean the horses?" he asked, with a smile.

She nodded. "Anything that gets people out and about, which also gives them the incentive to make it a goal and to go a little farther each trip. Pathways that don't have benches don't allow people to stop. But, if you put a bench out there for somebody who's struggling to walk, they'll make it that far, and then they'll collapse and decide whether they want to keep going or not. At least if you give them a place to rest, they'll spend that time reaching for a goal." She pondered it for a few moments and then added, "I think we should try a couple."

"I think it's a great idea," he agreed. "And that's the thing about this place. Everybody, including you, is trying to figure out how to make it better."

She smiled. "And I've been here long enough that it feels like home, and I care about what happens to the place," she murmured. "I know not everybody has that attitude, but I do."

"I certainly do." Dennis chuckled. "And people like us—whose work is rarely understood—can make a difference every time."

"Agreed," she murmured. "It's sad that nobody does understand all that we do to make our jobs work, but, at the same time, it's not why we do it."

"Exactly." He handed her an omelet.

"I didn't ask for that because I was gonna eat on the go." Yet she studied it, wondering if she could take the time.

"Maybe not," he noted, "but you'll still do better if you have food in your stomach. You think I don't know that you're always rushing and not quite getting the food that you need?"

"That's not exactly true," she argued, with a smile. "It's just that Saturdays are a little busier than others."

"This time, it sounds as if you need to take a moment and to not be quite so busy. And I just made it easy for you." He pointed. "Go grab a chair, sit, and take five minutes."

She laughed. "I will, but today only."

"Ha. You need to do it more often."

"I have a lot of work to be done," she murmured. "And it's not so easy to ignore."

"No, of course not," he replied. "We can't ignore the work. It'll just always be there."

"Always," she murmured, with an eye roll. But she obediently took the plate, grabbed some cutlery, and walked to a table close enough to talk to Dennis, if he wanted. "It's nice and quiet here in the morning, isn't it?" she asked, enjoying the taste of the hot food. She stared at the herbs, wondering what was so different about it. "What on earth did Ilse put in this today?"

"I think it's basil and provolone," he shared. "How is it?"

"Divine," she admitted. "But then the food here always is."

He chuckled. "And you make it sound as if it's a bad thing."

"No, not a bad thing," she disagreed, smiling. "When I'm here, I'm always aware of how good the food is. I hate to miss a meal."

"And yet you miss a lot," he noted.

"And that's mostly because I'm in here so early," she explained, "and you guys aren't ready with the food yet."

"But there's always other food," he pointed out. "You can have yogurt parfaits, granola. Plus you can have all kinds of prepared food, as the kitchen's always open. You know that."

"And I forgot how much of a worrywart you were," she teased in an easy manner.

"How could you forget that?" he asked in mock horror. "Here I figure I'm always around enough that people know what I'm doing."

"You are." She nodded and continued to enjoy her omelet, as she sat here in the peace and quiet. She looked over at him. "The guy who was here yesterday, Spencer? Do you know anything about him?"

"Nope, he just arrived. It'll take at least a day or so before I get to know him," Dennis joked, with a big grin. "After that, then he's mine."

She chuckled. "I'm surprised you give him that long to adjust."

"I'm not sure I give it to him as much as the others insist that he take it," he admitted. "And I know the adjustment can be bad. I did overhear something, as I walked past his room, with one of the doctors and Spencer discussing his head injury that's caused him quite some trouble. Neck alignments, missing ribs, the whole nine yards."

"And any one of those can be bad all by themselves," she noted. "The brain's a fascinating part of the body, but, wow, injuries there are tricky. Although he didn't seem fazed."

"Yep, we can't deal with severe brain injuries here," he

murmured. "Other specialized centers are for that."

She nodded. "And that makes sense. He didn't appear to be adversely affected in any way, so I'm happy for him."

"You seem to be interested in him."

"Curious," she corrected cheerfully. "I don't get as much exposure to the patients as you guys do. So, when I get a chance to sit and to visit, I always want to know more of the story."

"Of course. Spencer sounded interesting."

"They all do," she noted, as she looked around. "Again, I don't get that much hands-on interaction with the rehab patients."

"You can always do more in that arena, if you want," Dennis suggested. "No shortage of people who need help."

"I know," she agreed. "Dani's setting up more riding sessions, and I'm building a loading area, so that the patients can get up and down more easily, as they mount the horses."

Dennis stared at her in surprise.

She shrugged. "Just seemed to be a good idea."

"It's an awesome idea," he exclaimed. "See? I'm so busy here that I never even think about all that stuff. But that's what you're doing?"

"Yep, that's what I'm doing," she confirmed, with a wicked grin. "At least sometimes. The rest of time I'm mowing lawns and trimming hedges and regraveling paths and pulling out weeds and all that other stuff," she shared, as she got up and walked over with her plate. "And this omelet," she murmured, "was delicious. Give Ilse my thanks, please."

And, with that, Bella dashed out again. As she exited the dining room, Spencer stood awkwardly on crutches at the entrance. "Well," she greeted him, "you're an early riser too."

He shook his head. "I couldn't sleep. I was hoping there might be coffee."

She called back to Dennis, "Is that fresh coffee, Dennis?"

"You know it is." He poked his head up over the counter, took one look, and saw Spencer. "You looking for a cup of coffee, young man?"

"If possible, yes, please," Spencer replied. "I had a pretty rough night. I just wasn't sure what the protocol was on getting coffee."

"It's always available, not always necessarily as fresh if you hit the coffee urn," Dennis explained, "but we always have the coffee pods." He walked around the counter to join him and said, "Come on over here, and I'll show you how to brew your own cup."

Spencer looked down at Bella. "Thanks." And he awkwardly shuffled out of her way.

He was missing most of his right leg. Something she hadn't noticed yesterday. "No thanks needed. Dennis just gave me a beautiful omelet, so I'm in a generous mood."

"And when you're not?"

"When I'm not," she replied, "I'm scary."

He laughed. "I highly doubt that. You're much too nice to be scary." And, with that, he unsteadily made his way to Dennis. She watched to make sure Spencer was okay, and then she dashed off again. The last thing she wanted was for her crew to think she was slacking off, while they were all hard at work.

As she made it back outside, she immediately picked up a shovel and got to work. Yet her mind was on Spencer. He had been moving at least, but each movement had seemed hard, stiff, as if every step hurt him. Which she imagined it did. She didn't know all his history; matter of fact she shouldn't be privy to any of his history, unless he wanted to share it with her. Yet obviously, just being a patient in a rehab center meant he had so much pain in his body and in his soul. She didn't know if just the journey here had caused the pain either. It would take time for all of it to calm down and to be something he could live with. She hoped that he managed to improve enough to get the life that he wanted for himself. And, on that note, she focused on work.

MAKING HIS WAY back to his room on crutches, while carefully holding his half cup of coffee, was no small feat for Spencer. Even if it had a lid on it. But he knew he would need some caffeinated fortification for the day ahead. It had been nice to see Bella again.

"Fascinating name too," he muttered to himself. And yet he knew that no relationships were in his immediate future. There just wouldn't be the time or energy for such a thing. He needed to devote everything he could to living life in his own body again. Forget about dealing with somebody else.

As he sipped his coffee in his room, some of his uncertainty dissipated. Nothing like a cup of coffee to make you feel better. He looked at his iPad, trying to sort out his schedule, grateful that—at least for the next couple days—he wouldn't have to do too much because he just didn't feel up to it. When a knock came on his open door, he looked up. Shane. At least that's what Spencer thought his name was.

"Glad you found coffee," Shane said. "I wanted to see if you needed a hand to get to breakfast."

"I wasn't sure what to do," Spencer admitted. "I managed to get coffee, and I've just been sitting here ever since."

"Come on with me," Shane offered. "I have to spend some time with you after breakfast anyway. This way we can kill two birds with one stone."

Spencer stared at the crutches and winced. "If you say so. I used crutches to get there earlier, but I admit that I'm not sure I'm up for it again."

"I wasn't even expecting you to get there on your own," Shane noted. "So crutches this morning would have been fine, but let's take the wheelchair now, unless you've got a problem with it."

"Of course I have a problem with it," he replied, "but it is the lesser of two evils at the moment. So I will deal with it."

"Good man," Shane said.

Then Spencer slowly made his way into the wheelchair and added, "I can push."

"You can, but today you get service," Shane declared. "After that, we'll see how much you can do and see about getting you to do it as much as you can."

Spencer nodded. "Everybody here seems to be fairly friendly," he noted cautiously, as they made their way to the dining room.

"Of course they are, absolutely no reason not to be."

"Maybe there's no reason, but that doesn't mean that people will put themselves out to be nicer than they need to be."

"We pride ourselves on being a family," Shane stated, "and family looks after each other."

"They also throw each other under the bus," Spencer replied, without thinking first.

Shane burst out laughing. "Wow, nobody can hurt you quite like family, right? I gather you don't have too many good family memories."

"My parents both died when I was a baby. I was raised by my grandparents, mostly because duty wouldn't let them put me into foster care," he explained calmly. "But that duty is a very cold basis for a relationship."

"Oh, it can be very cold," Shane agreed. "Is that why you headed into the navy?"

"Partly," he murmured. "And then I was more comfortable there, finding a family I hadn't had before."

"Got it. Then you know what I mean about being a family."

"I do, indeed. And it has a nice ring to it."

"Always. And we don't just say it lightly," Shane added. "We believe it."

"And even nicer when that's the truth," Spencer said. "It also means, then they get into your business, and they get nosy, and they ask all kinds of questions you don't want to deal with."

Shane chuckled all the more. "Oh, so true," he admitted. "And sometimes you'll have enough of it, and other times you won't get enough."

"Got it." Spencer nodded. "I did meet one person a couple times now already. Her name was..." And he stopped, trying to think of it, hating that he even had to stop to remember. Then it came to him. "Bella. Her name is Bella."

"Ah, our head landscaper. She runs a team of gardeners for the center and keeps the place going for all of us, for all of our sakes. She's a lovely person."

"She seemed to be," Spencer replied, without too much inflection in his voice, at least he hoped. "I was busy telling myself that I didn't have any time or energy for a relationship and that I needed to put her out of my mind," he shared, "but, if ever I had a type, she's one who would fit mine."

At that, Shane looked at him in surprise. "That's an interesting take, and I'm glad that you're thinking about your needs and what you'll need in order to heal here," he stated, "because, in all honesty, we've had so many relationships bloom in this place, it's been fascinating to watch."

"Really?" He twisted in his wheelchair to eye Shane and then shuddered. "I need to remember to not twist."

"Yeah, all goes to that lovely head and neck injury. Besides, when you have a chance to make a friend here, it's valuable. Rehab can be tough on everybody."

"I know," Spencer murmured. "I made friends at the VA hospital, but they were all male. ... It's a very different energy having female friends."

"But it's good," Shane murmured. "It's all good."

As they pushed their way into the dining room, Spencer looked around. "It's way busier than when I was here this morning." In fact, dozens and dozens of people were here. "Also the noise." He winced. In fact a cluster of people were off to one side. And something small with wheels attached raced from one beaming person to the next. He did a double take when he realized it was a tiny dog.

"Do you have problems with noise?"

He dragged his attention back to Shane but couldn't tear his gaze away from the happy little dog. Then someone carried in another dog, a Chihuahua. "Sometimes, yes. ... Goes back to the injury. The ear canal."

"Of course," Shane agreed as he eyed him watching the dogs. "We can look at that too."

"You can look at it. Don't know what you'll see

though."

"You don't worry about it. I'll take a look," Shane repeated. "And, if we can do anything, you can bet that we'll do our darndest to improve it."

"Sounds good to me," Spencer replied, turning to look at him. "I think the doctors at the other centers just gave up, figured I was as good as I could be, and that was it. How I needed to adjust to this being my life now."

"I'm not real good with that," Shane admitted. "I always think there's room for improvement, no matter how far we've come."

Spencer laughed. "You and probably nobody else then."

"Doesn't matter whether nobody else agrees with me or not," he stated, as he wheeled Spencer up to the buffet line. "As long as we believe it, then we'll work toward it. This is a place of hope, not a place of defeatism."

"Glad to hear that." Spencer looked around at all the patients gathered here, but admitted to himself that he was looking for the little dog on wheels, but, to his disappointment, he found no sign of him. "How much hard work are we doing after breakfast? I need to know how much is safe to eat now."

"You tell me," Shane said. "How is the stomach? Speaking of stomachs, that little dog on wheels that you saw is Racer. And the Chihuahua being carried around a lot is Chickie. Both have very touchy tummies. So please don't feed them. That goes for all the animals on the place. Some have specialized diets that we need to be vigilant in respecting."

"Good to know about Racer and Chickie. As for mine? Up and down. Generally it functions okay, but it can get upset at the slightest thing, and I never understand why."

"Do you have any food allergies?"

"No, not that I know of—maybe some intolerances, but I don't know about that either," Spencer replied. "Food's always been there to sustain me. It's never necessarily been anything I thoroughly enjoy."

"Probably because you have a lot of stomach upset."

"I don't know what *a lot* is," he admitted, "but it's always been part of my life. ... I do love food though, when it's good."

"The food here is unbelievable," Shane noted. "So you eat what you want, and we'll deal with the consequences, and that'll give us a marker of how to go onward."

At that comment, Spencer looked at the sausages and bacon and Dennis's face and said, "Yes, please."

Dennis just chuckled. "Good. Healthy eating will get you back on your feet faster than anything, and, what we can't do in the kitchen, Shane here can do." And, with that, Dennis quickly ladened the plate full of eggs, sausages, bacon, and then asked if Spencer wanted hash browns. Finally, with a loaded plate on his lap, Spencer waited for Shane, who then grabbed a plateful for himself, about half of the food that Spencer had.

Then Shane pushed him forward a little bit, where they gathered cutlery. "I'll come back for coffee."

Spencer murmured, "I could use a second cup."

"Good enough." And Shane took him out onto the deck. "Are you okay in the sunshine?"

"Maybe not," he muttered. "It depends on the sun again."

Shane brought him back inside, so they were just beside the door, and asked, "How about this?"

"That'll work. It would be a shame to miss out on all

that sunshine."

"You've got time for that later, and you can bring sunglasses then," Shane suggested. "That'll make it easier."

"Good point." With that, Shane got their drinks and they sat to eat.

Shane and Spencer were quickly joined by several other people, and the conversations rolled around Spencer, as people discussed cases in generic terms and the weather and news. Everything and anything seemed to be okay. It surprised Spencer. A lot of times people didn't allow shoptalk in the community areas. But here, it seemed to be totally okay.

By the time Spencer finished eating, Shane had been sitting quietly, talking with a couple other people. Spencer usually felt the need to hurry, yet he didn't hurry much these days. When he finally put down his fork, he said, with great pleasure, "That was good."

Dennis heard his compliment, as he cleaned off a table behind him. He smiled. "I'm happy to hear that. Make sure you come back often. The only reason you'll starve in this place is if you don't let us know that something's wrong. Even if you're too tired to come to meals, I'm happy to bring you a plate or to get you food anytime."

"I wouldn't want to cause you any extra work," Spencer noted. "I think, most of the time, the staff are very underappreciated, particularly in the healthcare industry. It's so easy for us to just forget that you are people too. We go about our day, usually caught up in our own misery, trying to find a way to make our life easier, and you don't even become part of the equation."

Shane tilted his head. "That's an interesting take too," he noted, looking over at Dennis. "What do you think, Dennis?"

"I think he'll fit in just fine," Dennis stated, "because we all come from heart, and we treat our staff like gold because we know their value. We also treat the patients like gold because they are valued too." At that, he grabbed all the dirty dishes and quickly disappeared around the corner.

Shane looked at Spencer. "You ready to go?"

"I think so. I'm just a little nervous about what your testing might find."

"Not a problem. We'll just go over your chart, your past history, then take some current readings and sort out what we can do. I've already seen some of your previous X-rays, but I still need to go over them with you. Some of this I don't understand."

"I can't imagine that it would be easy to sort out," Spencer remarked. "I've had multiple surgeries, and I don't know whether you have the latest X-rays or not."

"I sure hope so," Shane stated, "Otherwise I'll be running you through the gauntlet to get them. I can't function if I don't have the latest and the best information. But you will know you better than anybody else, so we'll get you set up and on target as fast as we can. Let's head to my office, and we'll go over what I've got."

Chapter 4

THE NEXT FEW days followed the norm. Bella was busy fixing up several pathways that had shown some winter deterioration with the ground shifting. Thankfully Texas wasn't bad for that. This year hadn't seen the damage that had happened quite a few years ago, which was a blessing, because she always dealt with road maintenance and things to fix anyway, and she would contract out when needed, but she was ever mindful of her budget. And budgets always came around to bite her in the butt when it came to this stuff. It cost big money whenever she had to bring in certain types of labor. And anything to do with cement work or pavement was big labor.

She wandered, checking the fences for the horses and noting any weed piles on the inside. A few noxious weeds were always around that they had to keep down, but, so far, everything was looking pretty decent. As long as she could get these pathways tuned up again, particularly before she had to start on the heavy mowing, then she'd be happy. She had already ordered some benches and picnic tables for the yard. After the heavy mowing, she'd set them out.

She also had the lawnmowers to turn over and to do annual maintenance on. She'd sent several blades in to get sharpened and needed them picked up too. Plus they were short on shovels again, having had two men just break two sets of handles. It blew her away that they could do that so easily. But then, if you didn't understand how to use a shovel properly, you tended to use it as a pry bar. And no matter what she said or how she tried to explain it to these guys, they got it into their heads that she didn't have a clue as to what she was talking about, and somehow they knew better. It's one of the reasons she hated hiring contract laborers.

She wanted people who understood and were prepared to listen when she said something. Some of the guys were good, and some of the guys she could just do nothing about them. As it was, she had lots to keep herself busy for the next few days, and, if she didn't have to bring anybody else in, then she'd be happy.

She had a few guys always on staff who helped out, but they were also mindful of the fact that budgets had to be kept low, so, if she could do anything to keep the numbers down, she did so. Still, she didn't want to be the budget worrier. Dani always worried about budgets, but, when it was Bella's job on the line, she did what she could to make sure that things worked in the fields and in the books.

As she slowly worked away through the morning, she finally straightened up, wiped the sweat off her face, and looked at the others. "Who's heading into town to pick up supplies?" she asked. "I thought you were, Jerry," she called out to one of her regular staff.

"No, I switched with Ron," he replied. "He had to be in town anyway to pick up his son and to take him home."

She nodded. "Okay, good enough. Let's get this set of pathways here done. Lord knows we have a few more miles of them to do."

"If we could spray all this, it would help keep down the weeds, and it would stop the gravel from shifting as much."

"Yeah, but we have a lot of animals here," she pointed out, "so chemical sprays are not a good thing."

"We could stop them from coming out here?" he suggested hopefully.

"And that won't happen either." She chuckled. "There's a reason we have a veterinarian clinic here, and that's because it's full of animals. Remember?"

He nodded. "But we always have so many weeds to pull."

"And, if we don't pull them, they take off on us." She smiled. "And we have the time to deal with them."

"Not really," he argued. "We'll be mowing pretty heavily soon."

"Soon, but not yet," she replied cheerfully.

He just smiled agreeably and got back to work.

Most of the time he was great to have around; occasionally he got drunk on weekends and failed to show on Mondays. That was a pain in the butt when it happened, but everybody had something wrong with them, so she wouldn't argue with that. As long as he showed up 90 percent of the time, and he wasn't drunk at work, they were good to go.

"It's almost lunchtime," he called out about an hour later.

She stopped and looked at him in surprise. "Is it?"

He laughed. "You're the only person I know who can work so hard that you forget meals. I'd die eventually."

"I just hadn't realized how late it had gotten already." She frowned. "Go grab lunch then. I'll work a little bit longer and then go get myself something."

He nodded. "Good enough. See you back here in a bit."

He lived close by and often ran home for his lunch, which was another reason why he was always on target for lunchtime because he had family at home. His joy in life was getting to stop and see them in the middle of the day.

Not long afterward she walked back up to the dining room, grabbed a sandwich and a couple pieces of fruit, and walked out onto the deck.

Dennis joined her. "Good to see you."

She smiled. "I don't know how you can keep track of everybody," she said, with a headshake. "I have enough trouble keeping track of my three-man staff."

He burst out laughing. "Maybe they're very different things. You've got to remember. The kitchen staff is contained to one smaller area and can't exactly leave on me."

She chuckled. "My staff is always so anxious to run to town and to go on to the next thing."

"And sometimes you can understand that. I gather that was Jerry just leaving, wasn't it?"

"Yeah, he left a bit ago." She smiled. "He's a happy man when he can go home and have lunch with his family."

"And there are worse things to argue about in life," Dennis noted. "He's darn lucky to have a job where he can do that."

"I remind him of it often too," she replied cheekily.

He grinned. "I'm sure that goes down well."

She shrugged. "Even if it doesn't, it won't hurt to remind them all that a lot of perks come with their job here that they might not get elsewhere."

"Absolutely," Dennis agreed. "I remind myself on a regular basis too.'

She smiled. "Can you imagine working anywhere else?"

"Nope, I can't. It's a pretty special place to be."

"I know, and such an odd thing to consider that I ended up here," she noted. "I was working for the city and thought that I would be there forever. I was happy there. I enjoyed the work and was full-time."

"What happened?"

"My boss," she said, rolling her eyes. "He had sticky fingers and made my life one big mess."

"Sticky fingers?" Dennis repeated. "He used to steal?"

"I guess I should have said *roaming fingers* instead. He made it quite clear that the nicer I was to him, the better chances I had of getting more work from him."

"As if you'd want that," Dennis replied in disgust. "Too bad some guys can be complete jerks like that."

"Right." Then she tossed back her bottle of water and added, "Time to go." Before she left, she asked, "How's Spencer doing?"

"He's doing well," Dennis noted. "Maybe you should spend a couple minutes and find out for yourself."

"I haven't been avoiding him," she protested, "but I haven't seen him either. He was new, and I figured that he would need some time to settle in."

"He does. And he is," Dennis confirmed. "But I know he asked about you once too, so don't be a stranger."

She smiled and nodded. "Maybe I'll check in and see how he's doing later. I don't know what room he's even in or how to get a hold of him." She frowned.

He gave her the room number and added, "Just don't tell him that I told you that. And if I find out that you're being a pain in the butt …"

"Yeah, that won't happen with me." She gave him an eye roll.

"Exactly. Now go on. Get back to work."

She smiled and skedaddled.

SPENCER HAD TO wonder if that lovely Bella was avoiding him. Or maybe she'd been friendly but really had basically tripped over him, and now she was busy in her own world.

He had no reason to complain. She'd been a welcome sight when he'd first arrived, and even now, a few days later, Spencer found it hard to settle in.

Of course settling in was a different thing here. The place was alive in ways that the other centers he'd stayed at hadn't been. Hard to explain but here things were happening. Even if they weren't doing so in his world, he felt it, saw it around him.

He'd had more meetings than he'd expected to have. Doctors, nurses, psychiatrists, physiotherapists, and so many others, including Dani for some much-needed paperwork. He'd also gone over his medical history with most. That hadn't been pleasant, but now that they were done with all the initial tests, Spencer knew the hard world of rehab would start and soon. He just hoped it wouldn't be more than he could handle. Yet, at the same time, he could hope for more than he'd seen before, as it would show him that progress could be made here.

Everyone was so friendly and helpful that he'd been suspicious at the beginning. However, as he got accustomed to it, he realized how much nicer his days were in such an atmosphere.

But even that wasn't alleviating the fear of what was to come. How bad could it be? Surely not that bad. Shane didn't look gang-member tough or militant. Yet none of that made Spencer feel any better.

He hated that how he felt made a difference, but the first

day with a new medical team was always tense, as he figured out how to get along with a new system and with someone who had slightly different techniques. Spencer had a tendency to hold back and to watch and learn, instead of applying himself.

He didn't want Shane to see him holding back, but Spencer also knew what would happen if he did it after weeks of nothing.

Still, only time would tell how these early sessions would go. He hoped well but also knew they could go very badly.

Unfortunately he'd seen it all before.

Chapter 5

TAKING DENNIS'S ADVICE, Bella went through Hathaway House at the end of her shift the next day. She was later than she intended, and psychologically she wondered if she hadn't come deliberately a little late. She wandered through, looking for Spencer's room. And, when she came upon it, and nobody answered, she had to admit to being disappointed.

As she stood here, wondering what she should do next, she heard sounds of a wheelchair, slowly making its way toward her. She turned to see Spencer, looking as if his world were about to collapse and as if he were at the end of his energy. She bolted forward and then slowed her steps when he saw her.

He smiled. "I appreciate both the attempt to help me and the realization that I am making it."

"You are," she agreed, trying to hold back the anxiety in her voice as she studied him. "But honestly you look as if you're done."

"That's because I am done," he confirmed, with a muffled groan. "And I didn't think even being this done was possible."

"Sorry," she murmured.

He nodded. "It's all right. Sometimes you just need to know that you can't do anything more. You can try all you want, but, at one point in time, you're absolutely done."

"What is pretty amazing is that you're still here, even after the rehab horrors I've heard about."

He smiled. "Not a whole lot of choice. Either you deal with this now or it'll be in your face forever."

"So, hard pain at the beginning and a lot of gain at the end."

He looked at her in surprise and then slowly nodded. "That's the hope at least."

She smiled. "I'm pretty sure in Hathaway House that's as close to a guarantee as you can get."

"And I think you're right there, but it still takes a lot of trust to even see it happening."

"Oh my, I can't imagine. I've never had a major physical injury, such as you're dealing with, but I've seen a lot of people come through here. And a lot of them leave in much better spirits and physical states than when they arrived."

"I'm counting on it," Spencer replied, "even if it feels beyond impossible at the moment."

"Of course it does," she declared, with a vote of confidence. "And I'm so sorry. I gather you had a harder day than you expected."

"I think they'll all be harder days than I expected now," he noted, trying for a laugh. "Testing's done, actual sessions are now happening, and man, oh, man. I've got muscles I didn't even know had survived the accident." He breathed hard, as he rested in front of her, his arms on the wheelchair arms. "And it is okay for me to say that because I would fail terribly to make it look any better than it is today."

"You don't have to make anything look better," she stated calmly. "You do the best you can do each day, and that's all any of us can ask of you."

He smiled. "But who'll stop me from asking more of myself?"

She stepped out of the way, pushing his door wider, so that he could get in a little easier. "Have you thought about the hot tub yet?"

"Thought about it because I heard about it, but I haven't asked for access," he shared. "I'm not sure I can even get there and back on my own. It might be a waste of energy for anybody else to get me down there and back, when it'll probably take somebody on the medical staff, assigned specifically just for me."

"I would think it has to," she replied honestly. "Because of insurance, they must have somebody with everybody who goes."

He pondered that for a moment and then nodded. "You're probably right. Insurance is such a sticky business these days."

"Yeah, it sure is," she agreed. "Anytime you want, you can just ask for an orderly."

He shrugged, and she realized he would be the guy who didn't want to ask for any help.

"You know that absolutely nothing is wrong in asking for help, right?" she asked on a half laugh. He just smiled at her, and she realized that she'd hit it right on. "Let me put it this way. Anytime you want to go outside for a trip around to see the place, and you don't want to ask for help, give me a buzz." She pulled a page off her tiny notebook, wrote down her cell number, and handed it to him. "I can take you out and can give you a tour of the grounds." He looked at her in surprise. She shrugged. "It's beautiful here, and it's my work, so, of course, I'm proud to show it off."

He flashed a quick grin at her. "In that case, maybe, but

not today."

"Nope, not today," she agreed. "You seem completely done in. Time to crash or soak in a hot tub or whatever it is you guys do after a bad session."

"Today I'll crash," he murmured, "probably won't even make it for food."

"In that case, tell somebody," she suggested, "because, once Dennis finds out that you're skipping meals, he'll panic that you'll waste away to nothing." He stared at her to see if she was serious, and she burst out laughing. "I'm only partially joking. He is incredibly invested in everybody here."

"He hardly even knows me," Spencer protested.

"And that just means that he'll keep at it until he does," she added. Noting just how tired he was, she backed out of his room. "Didn't want to disturb you. Go ahead and just crash and do whatever. I'll see you around."

And, with that, she dashed off. Hard to even think about the impact that he had on her senses. Something was just so poignant about a man trying so hard to be strong and yet dealing with what seemed to be complete and utter failure in so many ways. It broke her heart, and yet she also wouldn't demean him by feeling sorry for him. Life had dealt him a tough hand, but he was handling it, and that was way more than a lot of people were doing. And she could only be proud that he was doing as well as he was.

SPENCER CRASHED ON the bed, his eyelids shut, until he heard a knock on the door. He called out, "Come in." Shane stepped in. At least he recognized Shane's voice.

"Hey, that bad, *huh*?"

"Yep that bad," he admitted, too tired to raise his eyelids, "at least right now. I keep hoping things will ease, and it will get better."

"It will," Shane noted calmly, "but I was worried you'd overdone it today."

"You think?" he quipped. "If you mean *overdone* as in still having some strength to get up and maneuver, I'm overdone. If you mean having done too much in that I'll never get out of this bed again? Yep, I'm overdone." Just enough self-mocking laughter filled his voice that he knew Shane wouldn't take offense.

"I don't want to see you guys crash so early into the rehab program," Shane explained. "Makes your recovery a lot harder."

Spencer opened his eyelids and stared at him. "I'm not sure what I was supposed to do differently."

"You weren't supposed to do anything differently," Shane replied. "I was. I shouldn't have let you carry on quite so far."

"Honestly I was good, until I stopped, and I shouldn't have stopped," he noted. "Because, as soon as I did, everything came crashing down, and all the muscles seized up. I even found it hard to breathe there for a while."

At that last comment, Shane was not happy, and he asked, "How about the hot tub?"

"If it means moving, no way," Spencer said.

"All it would mean doing," Shane explained, "is getting changed and getting into the wheelchair. I'd get you down there."

"Still seems to involve way-too-much effort." Spencer moaned. "I was thinking a shower, but I can't manage that either. And I'll tell you upfront that I can't manage dinner for sure."

"*Uh-oh*, in that case, I'll insist on the hot tub.'

He opened his eyelids again and stared at him. "Seriously?"

"Yep, if it's that bad, we need to ease up those muscles, before they lock down and seize up."

"I think you're already too late." He groaned again. "Just the thought of even moving is enough to make me want to cry."

"Definitely need the hot tub." Shane walked over to the drawers in the built-in closet, pulled out a pair of swim trunks, and asked, "Are these for you?"

He turned toward him and nodded. "I still don't think I can get there though."

"I'll have you ready in a jiffy." And, with Shane's help, Spencer was changed and seated in the wheelchair.

He looked at Shane in astonishment. "You've done that a time or two."

Shane laughed. "More than a time or two," he admitted. "A couple millennia worth and that's okay too. Makes the job a lot easier because I know what I'm doing."

"I hear you there but wow. Every time I think I can handle something, whatever else comes along just kicks me to the floor."

"And sometimes we fall and take pride in it," Shane offered, "but we don't do it for rookies, and we don't do it when you first get here."

And Spencer heard the regret in Shane's voice. "It's not your fault."

Shane raised his eyebrows and asked, "And whose fault is it?"

"Mine. I know what my body can do. I go-go-go, and

then I drop—literally."

"Now I know too," Shane stated, "so no repeat event."

"It's not that bad," Spencer protested, but they were almost at the hot tub. This was the first time he had seen this whole area. "Wow, I never did get a tour."

Shane looked at him in surprise. "Seriously? We always give tours in the first couple days."

"Maybe that was my fault," Spencer admitted. "A couple times people have knocked on my door, and I've just been too exhausted to even answer."

"That's quite possible then."

"And, of course, a very pretty lady offered me a tour herself today," he shared, with a smile. "So I'm okay if you guys skip it, and I just go with her."

Shane asked, "Who?" And when Spencer responded that it was Bella, Shane started to chuckle. "In that case you get a tour with her," he stated. "And if anybody is ready to show you the grounds, it should be her. She's put a ton of effort into them. I know she's immensely proud of her work here."

"In that case," Spencer added, "maybe I will because I wonder if anyone tells her that she is doing such a good job."

"I'm not sure," Shane replied thoughtfully. "That's the job that we don't see happening. We just see the results and think it happens without any effort."

"And yet the effort"—he waggled his eyebrows at Shane—"has got to be huge."

"It does. I'm glad that you two have hit it off."

"Sort of. She seems to be a cutie."

"That she is. She's also one of the hardest workers in the place. Been here quite a few years too," he acknowledged. "I don't know a whole lot about her though. It seems she's always working on an opposite shift to me."

"I can see that. She always seems to be around and about but probably not at the same time that anybody else is."

"And that's exactly it. We have so many staff members, and everybody's on different schedules to cover all twenty-four hours of a day, so you just never know who's coming and who's going, who's starting, who's leaving. And sometimes that's great, but sometimes it's also easy to lose track. I've known Bella for quite a few years, but I can only count a handful of times that I've stopped and had a cup of coffee with her."

"She doesn't seem to stop much," Spencer noted drily.

"Oh, you are not kidding. She has energy that you wouldn't believe. One of the times that I was attempting to visit with her out on the grounds, she just kept bouncing all over the place. I finally asked her what the problem was, and she said nothing. She just was high energy."

"She wasn't high-energy today when I saw her, but she's got something special," he admitted.

"She does. It's called love of life," Shane noted, with a smile. "Not everybody's got that extra something."

"No, no, that's for sure, but I'm blessed that she offered."

"And you should be," Shane agreed. "I don't know of any other person she's given that offer to."

"I'll text her and take her up on it."

"And she gave you her number?" he asked, waggling his eyebrows.

At that, Spencer smiled knowingly. "I'm a broken-down wreck. I'm pretty sure she thought I was harmless."

"And are you?" Shane asked him quietly.

"I am right now," he admitted. "Absolutely no idea what I'll be like when I get back on my feet."

"At least you're looking at that being a future possibility," Shane noted, "and that's good."

"Definitely feels as if there's a future for me. I just don't know what shape or form it'll take," he shared. "I keep hoping it'll be better than I'm expecting, but I also don't want to expect too much and be disappointed."

"Pick something that you want to deal with, something that you want to get back to, something that would make it seem as if you have arrived, fix whatever that needed to be fixed to reach that goal that confirmed you were there," Shane suggested, "and then we'll work toward it."

"*Hmm*," he murmured, as Shane helped him upright, until he was holding the rail of the hot tub, catching sight of the animals in the distance. The little llama had taken immediately to that family of horses. Something about her presence, fitting in with her new family, made him smile. "I don't even know what that would be." *Except maybe riding horses again.*

"And that's why I'm telling you now," Shane said. "We have weeks and weeks of rehab work to do. So I'm sure, in one of those sessions, something will pop up as that thing which you really miss, and we can drive toward getting that back into your life."

"Sounds good." And slowly—his body feeling as if it had aged hundreds of years just today—he moved his way deeper into the water of the hot tub. As it washed over him, his body trembled.

"You okay?" Shane's brows steepled, as he studied him.

"Yeah, I will be. I can feel the shakes too," he murmured, "but I think they're good shakes."

"Is there such a thing?" Shane asked in concern.

"I think so." Then he sank until just his face was above

water. And he let out a heavy sigh. "I didn't want to make the effort to come here, and I didn't want any more effort being expended on me," he explained, "but, man, now that I'm here? This was a good decision."

"Good," Shane commented quietly. "I don't want to see anybody suffer, and you were suffering more than you needed to. You're also allergic to a lot of drugs, aren't you?"

"I am," he confirmed.

"Severely?"

"I don't know what *severely* means anymore," he replied quietly. "Somehow it seemed severe at the time, but I don't remember."

"And how often have you tested them?"

"Some of them, I have quite the reaction," he shared. "Some of them are not too-too bad. Yet they're all on my watch list. I think only one gives me a rash. With others, I swell. One gives me blackouts." He shook his head.

"In that case," Shane declared, "we're avoiding them all. So the hot tub just might be where you need to come on a regular basis."

"Oh, gosh," Spencer murmured, a smirk on his face. "What a tough job."

"It is," Shane agreed, with laughter in his voice, "but somebody's got to do it."

Chapter 6

BELLA WORKED FURIOUSLY for the next few days, not necessarily by choice but because a lot of work was piling up. They'd had a flood from a leaking watering trough, and that had left them with a pile of mud to deal with that was being tracked everywhere. So they had to dig a drainage ditch and a pit to make the trough function properly, as it should. By the time she was done every day, she would eat and crash early after a shower.

However, a few days later, by the time she had a chance to take a breather, she realized that another day was basically done. She groaned, feeling her whole body and shoulders ache, particularly today. She'd been short one laborer, and, never afraid to pick up the tools required for the job, she'd been shoveling a little bit more than her body was happy with.

She pondered the hot tub, and, of course, that brought her mind back to Spencer, wondering how he was doing. Deciding that the hot tub would help her to function properly tomorrow, she got home, had a quick shower and changed into her bathing suit. She slowly put on a cover-up and hung a towel over her shoulder and headed toward the hot tub. Just as she collapsed into the water, she heard a chuckle beside her.

She surfaced to see Spencer. "Great minds think alike,"

she said, as she sank back under.

"Tough day?" he asked.

"Yeah, digging a drainage ditch."

His eyes widened, and then he winced. "Oh, lovely."

"Nope. Not. I don't think that vocabulary works when it comes to that."

"And why you?"

"Why not me?" she asked, with a note of humor. "I can't lift as much as the guys do, that's for sure, but I'm always there, doing my part. Besides, we were short-handed today, and it's not as if that's the only thing we had to do today."

"Of course not." He smiled at her. "Maybe you can just relax now."

"That's the hope."

"I didn't realize that you stayed here."

"Yeah, I was an early adopter, so, when an opportunity came, I moved in one of the on-site apartments. Nobody had to tell me twice. Fresh grub, and grub to be crazy about," she noted, "and access to all the grounds and not having to commute?" She just waved a hand. "I don't understand the people who have to consider whether it'll work for them or not. For me it was a done deal immediately."

He nodded. "It's one of the nicest places I've seen. Dennis told me about all the work you do. So has Shane, for that matter."

She smiled. "Both those guys have been here as long I have, even longer," she said. "And you'd think that we would have more time to spend and visit, but, no, we're always so darn busy."

"Shane did mention something along that effect, how he barely had a chance to sit and have coffee with you over the years."

"And he's right. Sometimes our schedule is off, or somebody's heading to town, or we've got other work to do, other people to look after." She smiled. "It's part and parcel of being here, and that's good too. You don't want to be so close that you see everybody all the time, and you don't want to be so far away and out of the loop that you don't know who all's here. Of course I never can keep up with all the patients who come and go," she noted. "However, I do try to keep up with the staff who come and go."

"And do many come and go?" he asked curiously.

"There's always a few. Some go and come back. Some go and realize they should never have left and then try to come back, but their positions are already filled," she noted, with a smile. "I've seen it all since I've been here. Been friends with a lot of them, and that's always been nice too. Some really good people are here."

He smiled. "And, of course, you're a cheerleader for the place."

"If I'm not, I should be," she declared. "Seriously, what's not to like?" She groaned, as she settled deeper into the water. "Especially on days like today. I don't have to maintain the hot tub. I don't have to pay for the expense of the hot tub. I don't have to do upkeep on the pool. All I have to worry about is getting my butt up the stairs for dinner." She grinned, her smile both elfin and brilliant at the same time. "How much of that sounds like a big chore to you?"

"Oh, it depends," he noted. "On the day that you saw me last, that was a bit more than I could manage."

"Did you stay in your room that night?" she asked curiously.

"No, Shane came just moments after you left and

dragged me to the hot tub. By the time I'd baked in here for a while, I went into the pool to chill out and did a bit of swimming. All under Shane's watchful eyes. Then I headed up and grabbed food. I didn't stay long, and I can't say that I was social," he admitted. "However, I was proud of myself on having made it."

"Oh my, you deserve a reward for that."

He chuckled. "Hey, I was just happy I made it there and back, without falling unconscious to the floor, and that I could get up the next morning."

"And it's all about the fight the next day that we have to watch out for. The reason I came to the hot tub tonight was I knew that, if I didn't do something to ease up my shoulders, tomorrow I would be suffering for it. Then I can't get the rest of my work done." She gave him a smile. "And so here I am. Taking care of business tonight, so that I can take care of business tomorrow."

SPENCER HAD TO admit he hadn't expected to see Bella, but was delighted he had. She fascinated him. And made him realize what he'd lost. She was fit and in a physical job, loving her outdoor work, being close to nature. It made him want to get back to his peak form even more. He completely agreed with everything that came out of her mouth. Particularly when it came to taking care of business the next day. He could have told Shane no, but Spencer also knew that he was better off coming to the hot tub, and he was.

Last night, when he had finished soaking in the hot tub, he'd gone into the pool, and that had been a refreshing shift yet again. He'd managed a few laps just to loosen up some muscles. Today? Well, the pain was almost as bad, but he was coping, and he thought that anybody who coped deserved an award.

Things were hard enough sometimes, and, if this was all that you could do, then that's all you could do. Nobody should knock it, and certainly nobody should make you feel bad about it. Yet he'd seen it all. He'd been trying to explain what was so different about the place to Timothy. And his buddy would be here eventually but not for another couple weeks yet, and Spencer couldn't wait.

He turned to Bella. "I'm looking forward to having a friend of mine come to rehab here as well," he shared. "He applied around the same time I did." Then he laughed and said, "I beat him to it." And he explained what had happened.

She chuckled. "You're just lucky you got in."

"And maybe because I had recommendations too." He wondered about that.

"I'm a big fan of *When it's meant to be, it's meant to be*. Don't knock it, don't ask questions, just accept it, and move on."

He burst out laughing. "A little bit simplistic, but I like it."

"Simplistic works," she declared. "You can rack yourself over until you're blue in the face sometimes, looking for a why. Often, there just isn't any why to be found," she stated. "And sometimes you're just better off to accept that."

He had to agree because, when it came to his accident, he'd tortured himself with the whys for a long time and then finally just gave it up, realizing that he would never find an answer. It had happened, and he needed to pack up and move on. And, if he couldn't do that, then there would be problems, bigger ones than he'd thought about so far.

"When Timothy gets here," Spencer added, "the two of you will get along fine. He's very much like me."

"Sounds good. People here need to mingle more. Everybody has something to offer, and we do tend to get locked into our crazy worlds and think that it's only us and only our world that's got anything happening. However, that's not true. Just so much is happening sometimes." She yawned. "And I know for a fact that they do all kinds of evening stuff here too, if you ever have the energy to get social."

"That hasn't happened yet," he admitted, with an eye roll. "Maybe one day."

She smiled and nodded. "And that day will happen sooner than you think," she stated, with a bright smile.

"We'll see." He laughed.

"Are you staying for dinner?" she asked him.

"I am, but it's always awkward. Do I go up there soaking wet versus going back to my room, getting changed, and then coming back again?" He shook his head. "Honestly, that whole process is exhausting."

She frowned. "I hadn't considered that. Yeah, I'd probably blow it off too."

"But then"—he held up a finger—"then there's Dennis's food."

"Ooh, you're so right. Dennis's food is worth getting out of bed for."

"Not only that, but, if I don't eat, what will tomorrow be like?"

"Yeah, do you wake up *hangry* too?"

"Yeah. And it's not, … not a great feeling."

"No, it's not." She sat up. "I'll dash into the pool for a little bit. You okay here?"

"I'm perfectly fine," he replied. "Shane checks up on me every fifteen minutes or so or sends down an orderly." She nodded, as he watched her small muscled body rise from the hot tub. She had on a bright red bikini, covering just enough and yet left enough to the imagination to make his blood boil. When she dove into the pool with a clean dive, he smiled.

"My kinda woman," he murmured to himself. He continued to watch her and then relaxed back into the heat, wondering how to make dinner happen and how to see if she was willing to go with him. But then, how was he supposed to get changed and get there at a decent time? When she suddenly appeared beside him, brushing the water from her eyes and dipping back into the heat, he asked, "Done already?"

"Don't want to overdo it. Just tired enough that I have to preserve my energy for tomorrow." She looked at him and said, "Tell you what. If you're happy here, why don't I grab food for both of us?"

He looked at her in surprise and then replied with real pleasure, "I'd like that, if we're allowed to."

"Not sure if we're allowed to or not," she noted cheerfully. "Still, as long as we don't go dunking our doughnuts in the hot water, I think we're probably fine."

He laughed, then sobered. "But then you can't carry it all."

"Either I'll shanghai somebody to give me a hand or I'll make two trips." She shrugged. "Either way, it's not an issue for me. We gotta eat." As she stood up, she asked, "What about any allergies though or preferred food choices for you? I don't know what's on the menu."

"Neither do I," he replied, "but I eat everything."

"Meat eater or veggie eater or starch eater?"

"Meat and veggies and a little bit of starch."

"Done. Back in a bit." And, with that, she was gone.

He'd been looking forward to dinner too. He wasn't sure what was on the menu, and now he realized it wouldn't matter one bit. It would taste divine, and no way he would make her feel bad by wishing she had gotten something different for him. He'd left it up to her, and he would eat whatever she brought.

When she returned a little later, carrying a large tray, Dennis was behind her, carrying another tray. Spencer laughed out loud. "When she told me that she would shanghai somebody into helping, I didn't realize she meant you," Spencer admitted. "Don't you have enough to do than catering to the rest of us?"

Dennis frowned at him. "Absolutely not, I don't."

And such seriousness filled his tone that Spencer didn't know what else to say.

But, for Bella, she burst out in peals of laughter. "You see? That's how it's supposed to be around this place," she declared, with a smile. "And Dennis figured that he might know a little bit about what you wanted to eat, so I left the food selections up to him."

Spencer sat up in the hot tub, pulled himself up so he sat on the ledge now, and a little table was brought over, and the trays were put down.

He looked at it and smiled. "Steak. Steak, baked potato, and Caesar salad. Man, was there anything more classic than that?" He looked over at Dennis. "Thank you so much."

Dennis grinned. "When you're ready for coffee, send her back up. Together we got this." And he was gone.

Spencer looked over at her. "Seriously, he doesn't

mind?"

"Seriously, he doesn't mind," she stated. "And I knew, if I went up there and told him that you were down here, he'd be here in a heartbeat. But that's Dennis for you. His heart's as big as he is."

"And that's a lot of heart," he noted, "because, man, that's a big guy."

Chapter 7

FOR THE NEXT several days that dinner remained in her memories, and Bella thought of it with joy. It's one thing to have a date, which that wasn't obviously, but it was another thing to come upon somebody in a natural environment and click as they had. And have everything work out. She was more impressed with Spencer than ever, and that was probably a problem because she shouldn't be even pretending to date somebody, especially not a rehab patient when they were at their most vulnerable.

She knew that there were certain rules about it in Hathaway House, but a lot of the rules had been relaxed over time, and she wasn't sure where any of that stood right now. She just knew that she really appreciated Spencer for who he was and for the trouble he was going through. And for the grace with which he was growing through it.

She never really thought about men and grace before, but it seemed to suit in this instance. And that in itself was odd. She'd had lots of healthy relationships over time, but nothing that ever stood the test of time. But she'd certainly seen the beginnings and endings of some patients' rehab efforts here, and she knew a lot of things could be said about somebody who faced trials, such as this.

She had come very close to getting married, only her partner at the time had walked a week before the wedding day. She'd been devastated. Her parents had not been impressed either, as they'd been stuck with some extra bills to pay, and he'd bailed because he'd felt he wasn't ready. *Wasn't ready* was the same thing as *cold feet* and didn't have any place in a wedding.

He needed to be well past that point before he ever reached one week before the ceremony. But he apparently hadn't been quite so interested in learning about who he was. When it came to his cold feet, it had hit Bella hard, and he'd booked it. She hadn't seen him since that fateful time. Not too long ago, she'd looked him up on social media and had been surprised to find that he was married with two kids. It blew her away because he had walked out on her only four years ago. So he'd obviously jumped into marriage very quickly with somebody else. Of course, then worry and fear had stepped in that maybe he'd been jumping before he split with her. She didn't want to take the time to go deeper into that and find out more.

No good would come of it, and it would just lead to more heartache and pain—something she wasn't willing to sign up for. It had taken her a while to even be friendly again with anybody else after that scenario, and her mom had urged her to get back out there and to find somebody new.

But Mom didn't seem to understand that finding somebody new wasn't the same thing anymore for Bella. She'd been totally in love with her fiancé. And it had been a shock to find out that he hadn't been anywhere near as engaged emotionally in their relationship as she was. She'd also been in love with the whole fairy-tale idea of the wedding, and, when that all blew up in her face, she hadn't had any fun taking things back and canceling everything.

She'd wondered at the time if maybe part of the grieving

process should have gone toward the actual ceremony. And that revelation made her feel very shallow, until a girlfriend of hers told her about how the wedding day was one of those special once-in-a-lifetime events that women really looked forward to. Bella had felt better after hearing that because it gave validation to how she'd been feeling and the depression she'd felt afterward.

And mostly because of his behavior then and immediately afterward, she couldn't even begin to think about trusting somebody else. She had finally gotten back out there but had never met anybody else who affected her the same way. And, of course, it was way too early to even contemplate that with Spencer. Yet, at the same time, she recognized his uniqueness, originality, and genuineness. And that meant a lot to her.

She kept working through the next day and the one after that. And when Friday came, she gave a *whoop*. The guys looked at her. She smiled. "I just realized it's Friday. And I'm off tomorrow." At that, they all started grinning at her.

"Right. It's been a long week."

"It has, indeed," she agreed. By the time they were done, and the tools were put away, she had to run into town to get more supplies, and she was already late for lunch when she returned. She raced up to the dining room to search for Dennis.

He took one look at her and pulled a plate out from behind the counter. "I was hoping you would make it back in time. I was going to give you another fifteen minutes."

"Hey, I appreciate it," she said, with a sigh. "Had to run into town to get supplies and, of course, had to deal with the traffic." She groaned, with an eye roll. "I just don't see it ever getting any better. It seems to get way worse every time I leave this place."

He nodded. "I haven't been in town for a couple weeks now," he noted, "and same thing. Every time I go in, I keep swearing I'm never coming back to town again." He had to laugh.

"And yet we do—for movies, clothes shopping, and-and-and."

"I know. It's one of those necessities that we hate, but, at the same time, when you're there, it's not so bad. Yet, by the time you're ready to leave for the day, you realize just how bad it's been because you're exhausted."

"And how can it be so exhausting?" she asked. "I mean, I spend at least all morning here, doing hard physical labor. However, when I go into town, in just a few hours, my soul's crushed."

He chuckled. "I'm sure that's an exaggeration."

She smiled. "Maybe a teeny-weeny one." She chuckled. "At the same time, it takes a special person to live in town, and I'm not that special person."

"And you've also made a niche for yourself here," he reminded her, "and so this is home."

"You're not kidding," she confirmed, with feeling. "The sooner I'm out of town, the better too. I just don't necessarily want to go the next time."

"Can't you send some of the staff?"

"Not this time," she explained. "I have to set up new accounts, and that always takes a little bit longer, and they don't have that clearance. And because most of them aren't long-term workers, I won't give that company information away. If we had accounts at some of the vendor companies, it wouldn't be bad," she noted. "But then I still have to give them a job which is one I could just do myself. So I left a little early, but then *leaving a little early* didn't quite do it as we were so busy in town anyway."

"Did you not eat at all?"

"I did have some granola for breakfast this morning, but that's it." She looked at the plate in front of her and grinned. "That salad looks fascinating."

"It's got fresh cranberries, raisins, and about four different kinds of seeds among lettuce of many varieties. Enjoy."

"I will," she murmured, as she took it outside. She sat down, her motion a little on the heavy side because she was so tired, and she just idled for a few minutes. At the end of the workday she was tired, but the weekend was here and hard to argue with that. As she tucked into the salad with gusto, Dennis laughed behind her.

"I do appreciate when someone enjoys their food."

"Hey, I always enjoy your food. Is Ilse around? I wouldn't mind a visit with her."

"She's in town herself. She's got supplier issues."

"Oh no, that's never a good thing, not when feeding all these people here."

"Nope, so she's gone in to talk to them herself. We're big clients and steady clients, but sometimes they need to have a little bit of a personal talking to before people get back into keeping prices in alignment."

"And especially when we're all on budgets," she noted, twisting slightly so she could see him.

He looked at the plate in front of her. "Did I give you enough?"

"You sure did," she replied. "I'll have trouble finishing it."

"And that's a good thing. You work very hard physically. I was a little worried that I hadn't given you enough protein."

She smiled. "When does anybody ever look after you, Dennis?" she teased.

He grinned. "One day there'll be somebody maybe, if I'm lucky."

And that was the first inkling she had that he was possibly looking for a partner too. She felt his pain because this guy was all heart. "It'll have to be a pretty special woman for you."

"That depends," he said, "whether it's someone else's version of *special* or mine. I don't want anybody interfering in my love life," he declared, with an eye roll.

"What? You mean, everybody here doesn't get a chance to get involved in yours, when you got so nicely involved with everybody else's?"

"Exactly. If everybody gets involved, it'd be way too confusing," he said, with a laugh.

"And nobody special is in your life right now, is there?" she asked curiously.

He shook his head. "Nope, not for a few years. Came close once, but she was killed in a car accident," he shared, with a gentle smile. "And for the longest time I just wanted to honor her memory. Then I realized I was hiding behind her memory." He shrugged. "Still, in the meantime, I haven't met anybody who makes me forget her."

"I don't think we're meant to forget them," Bella noted. "I think we're meant to honor them, to speak about them, to talk about them, to keep their memory alive by keeping them alive in our hearts and thoughts. Yet don't ever try to replace her because that's not possible."

He looked at her in surprise and nodded. "That's pretty deep for you."

"What?" she teased. "Am I not allowed to have all these deep thoughts that you seem to specialize in?"

He chuckled. "I do love a good philosophical conversation." He joined her, flipped a chair around backward, and straddled it to sit beside her.

"And enough people around this place get involved in some of those words of wisdom with you," she murmured. "I hear about it a lot."

"Do you?" he asked. "I never think about conversations making it out to the garden."

She burst out laughing again. "And you know perfectly well that I don't spend all my time in the gardens."

"No, I mean, you seemed pretty cheekily ensconced in that hot tub here what, a few days ago?"

"A little bit longer than that now." She smiled. "That was a really nice evening. I appreciated the help you gave us."

"Hey, you know how I feel about patients getting their needs met."

"I do, indeed, but not everybody does."

"No, that's true enough," he murmured. "Still, this place has done a lot for me, so I always want to give back."

"And you always seem to have that celebratory champagne at the ready now."

"And honestly I don't even put it in the budget. I buy that in town myself."

She stared at him in astonishment. "I'm sure Dani wouldn't have a problem if you did put it in the budget," she murmured. "I know she's a big fan of all the relationships that have happened here."

"She is, and so am I," he said, "but it doesn't have to be a company expense. I'm totally okay to make it personal."

She nodded, understanding what he meant. "It is pretty

special, isn't it?"

"It absolutely is," he declared. "Your day will come."

"And so will yours," she stated.

At that, he hopped up and walked back to his corner, carrying her empty dishes. "It will, but probably not anytime soon for me."

She wasn't too sure what that meant. But she was ready for a shower and maybe even a swim. As she wandered downstairs, she looked at the water, nodded to herself, and headed back to her apartment to get changed. When she came back, the pool was empty, which was just perfect. She just dove in from the side, and, although she'd already worked a lot physically today, she did several lengths and finally ended up with a good forty minutes of straight, steady swimming.

When she was done, her muscles were relaxed, almost like melted butter over thin toast. She pulled herself up onto the side, grabbed her towel, walked over to the closest lounge chair, collapsed, and basically stretched out and closed her eyelids.

And that's where she was, when a man spoke beside her.

"Look at that," he murmured. "This place even comes with built-in mermaids."

BELLA RAISED HER eyelids to find Spencer sitting in his wheelchair beside her. "I don't know about that," she argued, with a sleepy murmur, "but I am definitely one tired gardener."

He smiled. "You overdid it again, *huh?*"

She chuckled. "Isn't that my line for you?"

"Seems you're the one who overdid it though," he said, with a headshake. "You know better than that."

"I do, but going to town exhausted me." She smiled at him. "Still not quite sure how that works."

He shuddered. "Traffic, pedestrians, people, road rage. It's enough to make anybody scared."

"Yeah, even you, a big tough guy, *huh*?"

"Absolutely. I'd stay out of town as much as possible, if I could."

"You seem to have done a pretty good job of it by staying here."

He grinned. "Yeah, convenient, isn't it?" He laughed. "But still, some days, everybody has to brave that wild, wild west and head into the city."

"And to think that some people enjoy it."

"I've heard that. I haven't seen any proof of it yet though. Seems that everybody here has the same attitude."

"A lot of us do." She gave him a gentle smile. She yawned just then and covered her mouth. "Wow, I came in late, had a bite to eat, then decided on the pool. Probably overdid that too." She frowned, looking at the water. "And now I'm just tired again."

"You are always tired. You just never had a chance to get *un*tired."

She burst out laughing. "You've got a point there. How are you doing? I haven't seen you for a few days."

"Nope, it's been pretty busy in my corner too. Shane is not an easy person to work with."

"Oh?" she asked in concern. "Are you doing okay?"

"I'm doing fine, but there's no slacking when he's around."

"No, I don't imagine there is," she agreed, with a nod,

"but still, you don't want to overdo it either."

"No, I don't. Yet, at the same time, that's why I'm here—to get whatever rehab and recovery I can get from this place, and then who knows where and what I'll do after this?"

"And what do you do?" she asked. "I guess that's always one of the questions—when you're done here, where do you go, and what do you do then."

"I'm at loose ends. I was on the base in Coronado, California, where I got injured, but I do have extended family not all that far from here that I would like to get to know better, now as adults. So it'll depend what my next step is."

"And what would that be?"

He shrugged. "I'm a strategist, so it'll entail either economics or math."

"Wow, one of those brainy people, *huh*?"

"My biggest concern when I was injured," he murmured quietly, "was about my head injury. Considering the work that I've always wanted to do, it could have been catastrophic."

"And yet didn't you get a brain injury? Didn't you say something about that?"

He frowned. "I had head injuries, and I guess you could call that a brain injury. I was certainly … They took the top of my skull off to ease the pressure and to let some of the injuries heal," he explained. "There doesn't appear to be any lasting damage, and, for that, I'm grateful."

"Wow. I don't think that happens very often." She looked at him in surprise.

"No, I don't think so, and, in this instance, it's all good."

"So what would you do?" she asked. "I mean, I've never

heard of anybody doing strategy stuff."

"An economics position," he suggested, "which I'm not sure that I want to do as a civilian. I was even thinking about teaching again."

"Teaching again?"

He nodded. "I did a certain amount of teaching and business training before I went into the military, but I was young and didn't know what I wanted to do back then."

"So you are one of those superbrainy people?" she asked, a kernel of suspicion forming on her face.

He gave her a lopsided grin. "Does that mean I'm no good if I am?"

"It definitely makes you unique. I've never been terribly brainiac in any shape or form," she admitted. "I'm all about plants and nature and things." She gave a wave of her hand.

"So am I," he noted. "I went into the service to do that. To be of service. And I know that made me an oddity too."

"In many ways, yes, but good for you."

He smiled. "When you are touted for your brains, you often lose out on opportunities."

She stared at him in surprise. "And here I thought all those kinds of opportunities would have been a benefit. Instead, from what you're saying, it seems almost a hindrance."

"In many ways it was a hindrance. In many ways it opened doors, but not always the doors I wanted to open. Just because they were opening and seemed to be great opportunities, I could walk through them. However, I still lost out on a lot of other experiences. That's one of the reasons I joined the military. I wanted to get out from the economics world, where everybody saw me as who they wanted me to be, and instead I went to where I could just be me."

"I think you succeeded," she noted.

He nodded. "Yes, I did, and then I got injured."

"Ouch, talk about a way to stop a career."

"I was leaving anyway," he noted. "So time to get back to my regular life."

She smiled. "So joining the military was a sidestep for you?"

"I wanted it," he replied. "I wanted to do more for my country and to do more on a physical level. When you're hired for your brain but not necessarily super physical, everybody slots you into being the last pick on various sports teams. You never have the fun stuff that all the jocks do."

"I understand that. I was always the jock at school, and we had a blast. But you're right. So many people never got a chance to do what we did because we were all so good at what we did."

"Exactly, and, because I was so good at what I did, you can guess where my world ended up."

"Yep, exactly," she murmured. "That's fascinating." She studied him. "And what are you doing now?"

"I came for a swim," he said, pointing at his swim shorts.

"And yet instead you got stopped, talking with the hired help."

He leered at her. "If you're the hired help, this place is dynamite." And, with that, he shuffled his wheelchair over to the side of the pool. "I'll see you in a little bit. I need to get refreshed from some of Shane's rehab work, get the muscles relaxing a little bit."

"You'll go in the hot tub afterward?"

"I hope so. As long as it's pretty empty, I will be. If I can find someone to supervise."

"I can supervise. It's 100 percent empty right now."

"Yeah, but you know how that works." He chuckled, as he slipped into the water. "Give it ten minutes, and there won't be sitting room." And he went under and started working on his strokes. He was a huge swimmer, and, of all the sports that he would love to do on a much broader scale, it was swimming. He needed to add that to his goals list with Shane. Spencer could have been a professional swimmer; he knew that. But how did one make that choice when it was drilled into him all the time that he should do something with his *gift*, whatever that gift was in their mind?

It had been hard in many ways, but it had also been rewarding. He had done a lot of good things growing up that other people never had a chance to experience. Yet, at the same time, he'd also lost out on a few. After he did twenty laps in the pool, he made it to the side steps and bumped himself up until he was sitting at the top step.

He looked over to see her lying there, calm and just half asleep. Pretty decent that she could do that. Just be here at the end of her day, enjoy the evening, and be herself at the same time. Maybe a little bit of jealousy arose in him. Because she got to stay here permanently, where he was a visitor, and he would have to leave.

Interrupting his musings, an older man carrying—carrying what?—walked toward him.

Stopping in front of Spencer, the older man grinned and said, "Want to say hi?"

"I'd love to but what is it?" He studied the liquid furry form in surprise but willingly held out his hands to receive the soft animal. Its eyes looked at him inquisitively.

"Hey, Stan." Bella nodded at him, a big grin on her face. "Is that Pika again?"

"It is," Stan confirmed. He studied Spencer. "Pika comes every so often for some dental work. She has a bad habit of getting in the hard candies her owner refuses to give up. She's a four-year-old ferret."

Fascinated, Spencer cuddled Pika. "She's adorable."

"She's got a great personality. I like to bring her out to visit the residents at Hathaway, as she's very friendly to new people."

"She's adorable." Spencer's voice thickened with emotions, as he carefully handed Pika over to Bella. Pika immediately crawled up her shoulder as if recognizing her.

"Hey, Pika. How's my girl?" she whispered against her soft fur.

"You haven't made it down to my clinic yet." Stan made it sound more like an accusation.

"That's more my fault." Bella smiled up at him. "I should have taken Spencer there before now. We haven't even taken him for a proper tour yet."

Stan reached out his arms, and Pika raced into them and up onto his shoulder. "Anytime you need a pick-me-up, come on down. We always have someone around for you to cuddle."

"Sounds like a great offer," Spencer said immediately. "Thanks for letting me know."

"I'll take you down there later, or if you get a chance, you can always go on your own," Bella urged.

They watched in silence as Stan walked over to someone else to fall in love with Pika.

Dani had built quite a place here, and Spencer kept meaning to tell her that, but, so far, he hadn't gotten around to it. He'd been telling Timothy all about it, and, of course, waiting for his friend to get here was taking what seemed forever. He wondered what Timothy would think of Bella. Yet Spencer already knew that Timothy would think she was phenomenal and gorgeous.

If she were available, he'd make a play for her. Even though Timothy's body was twisted, and Spencer was dealing with some other issues himself, just enough of that light in Timothy's eyes always said that he appreciated the ladies. He was a ladies' man in some sense but honorable at all times.

Spencer made his way over to the hot tub by hitching his butt across the tiles. When he got to the other side, he heard chuckling. He looked over at her. She'd been watching his progress. "Hey, one of the things that you learn is that necessity is the mother of all inventions," he told her. "The thought of getting back into the wheelchair and making my way over and getting out of the wheelchair again?" He shook his head. "Nope, this was by far easier."

"Oh, I'm not laughing at you. I'm very appreciative of everything you do because you show me so much," she admitted impulsively. "A new perspective on old issues."

He looked at her in surprise. "Are you sure you're talking to the right person?"

She smiled. "Absolutely."

Chapter 8

JUST WATCHING SPENCER make his way, totally unconcerned about how anybody else would view it, made Bella smile. He was a really good guy. She walked over, dipped her toe in the water, and announced, "I'll go back in the cold water first." And she turned and headed over for another set of laps. By the time she was back at the hot tub, she was yawning the whole time.

"Seems to be bedtime for you."

"Nope," she disagreed, with a smile, "but it'll be dinnertime soon and then an early night. That's the thing about getting up so early in the mornings. Even on a Friday night, bedtime is still at nine o'clock."

"What time do you start in the morning?"

"Usually I'm already working at five a.m.," she shared. His eyebrows shot up. She nodded. "It's the coolest hours to be working, and it can get blooming hot out here, doing the work I do."

"I understand," he agreed. "I just didn't realize it was that early."

"No, most people don't," she confirmed. "It's also why my meals get skipped, as I am out of sync half the time with the kitchen."

"Got it," he murmured.

"I haven't had dinner, if you want to go up together."

She paused. "I think you still have one problem," she added. "You're soaking wet again."

"Right. It's a little early, I think. I probably have time to get changed beforehand. What about you?"

"We can do that," she noted, "if you're up for it. Maybe go and get changed and meet back in what? Thirty minutes or so?"

"I'll be done faster than that," he replied. "So, if you were being generous for my sake on the time, don't worry about it."

"I was being generous," she admitted, with a guilty shrug, "but that's all right. If you don't need all that time, I can probably get done that fast."

He grinned. "In other words," he murmured, "you're the one who needs time."

"I'll shower, wash my hair, probably put it in a braid, get dressed." She thought it over and then nodded. "How about we make it twenty minutes?"

"Good enough." She waited until he had repositioned himself back into the wheelchair. She hesitated to ask if he needed help, but he already read the thought on her mind.

He waved at her. "Go on. It's all good."

Still hesitating, but he seemed determined, so she turned and headed to her place. The thought of even dinner with him was enough to make her pick up her footsteps. She didn't want to be late. He's the one who had the excuse, not her. But she did have to shampoo her hair and get changed, and, by the time she was dressed again, she was running through her twenty minutes pretty fast. It just amazed her how quickly the time went by.

When she entered the dining room, she saw no sign of him. She looked around and waited off to the side for him to show. When another ten minutes passed, she wasn't at all certain what to do and then decided that maybe she better go check on him.

As she walked toward his room, she saw no sign of anyone at the room itself. She knocked on the door, and, when there was no answer, she hesitated. When Shane came up beside her, she asked him, "Have you seen Spencer recently?"

"Last time I saw him was in the pool."

"Me too. We arranged to meet outside the dining room for dinner in twenty minutes, and that was twenty minutes ago." Shane's eyebrows shot up at that. She nodded. "I knocked on his door, but he's not answering."

He immediately said, "I'll check on him." And he stepped inside, shutting the door on her. She heard the shout for a doctor from inside the room, and her heart slammed against her chest. She wanted to open the door and burst in, but she hadn't exactly been allowed to.

Then came a series of alarms, and, with her heart in her throat, she stepped out of the way, as people rushed into Spencer's room. She couldn't stand the thought of something going wrong or this very kind, gentle man hurting. Yet something had happened, on the other side of that door, that she didn't know about.

Three different people went in. When Dani entered the room and then came back out again, she walked over to Bella, her arms open to give a hug, and said, "He's fine."

Bella stared at Dani, tears in the corner of her eyes. "Dear God," Bella asked, "what happened?"

"Seems he fell," Dani murmured. "Unfortunately that happens a lot. He also clunked his head on the way down."

The tears threatened to overwhelm Bella, and she tried to wipe them back. "Good thing I came to check on him," she whispered. "We planned to meet for dinner. When he didn't show, I waited and waited, until I came by to see if he was okay."

"And it's a good thing you did," Dani murmured. "He is back to consciousness, but we'll keep him under observation overnight." She put an arm around Bella and led her toward the dining area. "You won't see him tonight," she noted, "so maybe go eat your dinner, and I'll send you a text later to let you know how he's doing."

At that, Bella took a deep breath. "Okay." She twisted to look at his door, still closed. "But you're sure he's okay, right?"

"We have doctors here and X-ray equipment. They'll check him over and see if anything is seriously wrong. Not to worry," she said. "We will look after him."

And, with that, Bella had to be satisfied. She stopped and gave Dani another hug. "Thank you."

Dani whispered, "You're welcome. It's a good thing you came and checked on him. It could have been a little bit longer before we found him, and, in cases of falls, it's always best to find them as soon as possible." And, with that, she turned and walked briskly back down the hallway, leaving Bella to head to the dining room alone.

SPENCER OPENED HIS eyelids, the room blurring in front of him. "What happened?" he whispered to Shane, standing over him, beside a doctor Spencer didn't recognize. Such concern was on their expressions that Spencer knew something was wrong.

"You either fell or passed out and then hit your head on

the way down," the doctor explained, while still checking Spencer's head. "And, although you have a hard noggin, you appear to have a concussion."

"Is that why there are two of you?" Spencer groaned, as the doctor pushed gently on his temple.

"Absolutely. And now you get to spend the next couple days resting. No more rehab therapy and I don't want you trying to get anywhere for a while, not until this calms down." He stepped back and glared at Spencer, but his voice was gentle when he added, "Do you understand me?"

Spencer stared at him, trying to comprehend what just happened. Surely the doctor wasn't serious, was he? "It's just a small head wound surely?"

"For the moment, but we don't want that simple injury to become something much worse. So bed rest and under observation all night. No arguments." With that, he made a few notes on his tablet, then turned and walked out.

Spencer couldn't believe it. With a side glance at Shane—who was also on his tablet, writing notes himself— Spencer muttered, "Seriously?"

"Absolutely," Shane declared quietly. "Head wounds can be serious. Do you know what happened?"

He frowned, thinking back. "Honestly no. I think I was in a hurry to get changed and just fell."

"Why were you in a hurry?"

Heat washed over his face. "To meet Bella in the dining room."

Shane chuckled. "In that case I understand the urgency, but next time make safety the primary concern."

"Yeah, I will. I missed my meet-up now I presume."

Shane smiled. "Absolutely you did. And you won't be meeting her for a couple days now."

Spencer muttered a curse word.

But Shane heard it, and, with a full chuckle, he added, "I wouldn't worry. She'll be there when you get back on your feet." And, with that, he left Spencer to his thoughts.

Two days in bed?

No way.

And not after missing an evening with Bella. He needed to get back on his feet and fast.

Chapter 9

BELLA BARELY SLEPT all night. She'd heard from Dani earlier in the evening that Spencer was awake and conscious, but the depth of her pain on hearing that he'd been hurt—and not even knowing fully what was going on or why—had sent her world in a tailspin. So unlike her. She'd certainly met a lot of people here and some who had more than a few injuries over time, but her response to finding out about Spencer had really thrown her.

When she got up this morning, she was more than a little on the shaky side. But she went to work, determined to put in a proper day, and yet kept glancing at her watch.

As she walked upstairs to the dining area, Dennis looked at her in surprise. "Are you working on a Saturday?"

She shrugged sheepishly. "I forgot. I went to work on that one path that I'd left yesterday and didn't even think about what day it was," she admitted. "But I couldn't leave it alone, not after hearing about Spencer getting hurt last night. So here I am. I came to get coffee and something to eat. Besides I often work Saturdays, so it's no biggie."

"Good thing, considering it's not a workday."

"And yet for you, you're here," she noted, with a smile.

"Yep, I'm not here all the time anyway though," he murmured. "And he's fine, you know."

"Is he?" she asked hopefully.

Dennis smiled and nodded. "Yes. He'll be fine, put it that way. I'm not sure I have all the details, but word travels fast around here. Spencer did fall, and he did bang his head, and he's definitely not doing anything for the next couple days, while he recuperates."

She nodded. "Have you seen him this morning?"

He shook his head. "Not even sure that he'll be coming for food," he murmured. "You want to go check on him and see what he needs?"

"Yeah, I was looking for an excuse to do that." She laughed.

"There you go," Dennis said. "No excuse needed now."

She smiled, picked up two coffees—Spencer's black and hers doctored the way she liked it. Then, walking carefully with both of them in her hands, she headed to his room. When she got there, she hesitated because carrying both coffees made it a little hard to knock.

She called out, "Hey, you awake?" A gruff response came from inside. Balancing the cups in one hand, she opened the door and poked her head around. "I brought coffee, but I wasn't sure if you were awake or not."

"I'm awake." He then shifted in the bed, while she watched. He smiled at her. "Coffee would be lovely. You really don't have to, you know."

"You keep telling me that," she replied self-consciously. "All I can say is, when I heard you got hurt, you've been on my mind. So this is an excuse to make sure you were okay."

He looked at her in surprise, and then she watched pleasure cross his face. Such a simple thing to tell somebody that they cared and that they were loved. She stepped in and placed his cup on the little side table and then moved it over so he could reach it. "Dennis wasn't sure if you would make it down for food either," she added.

"Does Dennis work weekends too? I always see him there."

"He's not supposed to, but he's a bit of a workaholic," she murmured. "I know there's a plot within the group to find him a partner."

Spencer chuckled. "A partner would probably be good for him," he murmured.

"I think so too," she agreed quietly. "We all need to know that somebody out there cares. So, if you want breakfast, let me know, and I'll tell Dennis."

"So now you're the errand boy too?" he asked in a teasing voice.

And she could appreciate the teasing, but, at the same time, she also saw the pain in his facial expression. "Any idea what happened?"

"Yep, I got up too fast and fell and banged my head," he shared. "I guess I was out cold for a little bit."

She nodded. "I'm the one who raised the alarm."

He winced. "Right, we were supposed to have dinner."

"We were," she said. "And then I felt terrible, thinking it happened because we put a time frame on it."

He chuckled. "No, it was just me and my clumsy lack of coordination."

"Maybe." She shook her head. "I think you're … You've been doing incredibly well here. I wouldn't want to put that added pressure on you."

"Not to worry. I put it on myself all the time."

"I think we're our own worst enemies many times," she said, "and, even here at Hathaway House, it can be deadly. You see so many other people doing well, progressing at a speed that you think you should progress at. So we push ourselves to do more, to do it faster, and often that doesn't work out so well."

He stared at her. "That's pretty insightful."

"Hey, I'm trying." She snorted. "I'm not Dennis or Dani by any means," she replied, with a bright smile, "but even I can see what happens at this place. And some of it's sheer magic, and other times it's just hard on everybody—or at least on those who don't have the same level of progress. I imagine the comparisons are devastating for them."

"I would think so," Spencer agreed. "I'm doing okay so far, and my friend's coming next week finally, after his arrival was pushed back. So, of course, I've been hoping to push myself a bit more, so I can show him how far I've come." Spencer laughed. "Yet that's foolish too because I can only go so far, and, if there's one thing that I have learned, it's that my body will make that determination, not my mind."

"And yet don't you think your mind leads the way?" she asked. "Don't you have to mentally imagine success in order to reach it?"

"Some say that," he noted, looking at her thoughtfully. "Can't say that I've ever had a chance to prove it."

"I think the theory is to visualize it in order to see the goal in order to make it happen."

"I'm not against that," he replied. "I think any tools that we have are tools that we should utilize. And some tools work better for some people than for others. It's all about trying and finding something that works. For me."

"Yeah, I agree with that." She nodded. "And just because you do try doesn't necessarily mean it's not working."

He smiled. "No, that's quite true as well. I think it's all about doing whatever you can do and being okay with it, even if you can't do it all."

She moved the table over a little bit, as a hint for him to drink the coffee. He picked it up and smiled. "I saw that little nudge."

"Hey, it's hot," she explained. "I can't stand cold coffee."

He burst out laughing. "A lot of times in my life I was very grateful for cold coffee and pretty glad to have it."

"And this isn't one of them," she stated firmly. "We're perfectly capable of drinking hot coffee and enjoying it while it is hot."

"And what if I like cold coffee?" he protested, but he picked up the cup, mindful of the wince on her face when he mentioned that. "How many times have you forgotten coffee and drank it anyway?" he murmured.

"Too many times," she admitted. "One of the reasons I try hard not to anymore."

He chuckled. "Not that that works for everybody."

"No, sure doesn't. Chances are it works for very few, who haven't really cared about it in a long time. Or they're just desperate to have the caffeine hit," she added cheerfully.

He nodded. "And that's possible too."

"So what do you want for breakfast?" she asked, as soon as her coffee was gone. "I'll pick it up."

"Will you bring yours back with you?"

She hesitated and then said, "Sure, why not? I'll tell you what I did do this morning that was pretty foolish." And she shared her story with him.

He chuckled. "If you've already worked today, then you shouldn't have to do errands." He hesitated, as if not sure that he wanted to send her off after breakfast.

"If I don't get you breakfast, then you can bet that Dennis will be here. So which is the worst-case scenario?"

He winced. "Fine," he agreed grudgingly. "But I'm really

okay, you know."

"Were you planning on getting up today?"

He winced. "I'm not sure I'll be given that option."

"Exactly, so let's make it easy on everybody. Now, what do you want?"

By the time she got his order and made it into the dining room, already a line was starting to form. When Dennis saw her next in line, he asked, "How is he?"

"He's doing pretty well. He's awake. He's functioning. He wanted to come himself, but I guess he's been given a warning," she shared, with an eye roll.

"Of course he has." Dennis smiled. "And so they should have."

"So what can we get?" By the time she had a rather laden tray full for both of them, she was staring at it, wondering if she could manage to carry it all. At that point Shane popped into the dining room and saw her heading out.

"Ah, good. I'll help you with that. I wanted to check on him anyway."

"As long as you don't upset him. It took me a bit to get him to let me deliver his breakfast."

"Pride is a hard thing," he murmured.

"So is falling and hitting your head," she stated equally as bluntly.

He burst out laughing. "You're good for him."

"Actually I think he's good for me," she corrected. "It's kind of an odd thing."

"What is?"

"Just how much I'm learning," she admitted. "I've only been interacting on a superficial level with the patients—the odd person I see when I'm out working, talk to for a few minutes, that kind of a thing. I'm never involved, but I am with Spencer. Not sure it's a good thing for him, but he's definitely an interesting character."

"Good. Come on then. Let's get down there and see what he thinks of my ruining his breakfast."

"He won't think much of it at all." She chuckled. Even with the two of them, it took a bit to maneuver the door open. She hit the button on the wall and muttered, "I should have seen this earlier."

Shane laughed. "I tend to forget about it too, but it's definitely helpful."

As they walked in, Spencer shifted in the bed to sit up. He looked at Shane in surprise. "She's pretty good about getting help, isn't she?" he stated. "I'm forever telling her that it's too much for her to carry, and, next thing I know, somebody else is there to help her."

"That's us," Shane noted cheerfully. As he set the tray on the table, Spencer took one look at the food, and his face lit up.

"I didn't think I was all that hungry, but now that you're here, wow, this looks awesome."

"I wasn't exactly sure what to get you," she confessed. "Once again Dennis saved the day."

"You guys are doing just fine." Spencer reached for a fork. "And I'll enjoy this." And then he stopped, looked over at Shane, and added, "I will, providing you won't run me through some tests and turn off my appetite."

"Oh, heavens no." Shane chuckled. "I'd hate to do anything to disturb you."

"Good, I would too." And he added, "Before you ask, I'm feeling fine, have no headaches, and I've been up to the bathroom, and all's good." He looked over at Bella. "Sorry for all the TMI comments, but I just happen to know the run of questions to expect from Shane here."

"As long as you know they're coming," Shane noted, "it shouldn't cause a problem."

"No, it doesn't cause a problem. It's just one more of those things that reminds us that our life is not our own here."

"But it's not far off," Shane argued calmly. He ran through his chart, noting that the night-time nurse had been in pretty steadily to check on him. "Seems you had a decent night."

"I did," Spencer confirmed. "It was a stupid fall, and I'll be glad to get past it."

"We all will," Shane noted quietly. "As long as there's no more to it, you are good to go. However, you'll stay and rest all day. Preferably in bed, and, when you want to get out of bed and do something, buzz me."

"Don't you guys ever rest?" Spencer asked sheepishly. "It is a weekend, you know."

"It is and believe me. Some of us would enjoy having that weekend."

"Ah, so, in other words, stay in bed, where nobody has to come and help me." Spencer laughed. "Got it."

"Some of us are here on call, regardless whether it's our shifts or not," Shane shared. "And you're part of my roster, and I take that very seriously." And, with that, he lifted a hand and was gone.

"He meant that, didn't he?" Spencer asked, as he looked over at Bella.

"I think so," she replied. "I think it goes for all of them. I bug Dennis about being here seven days a week sometimes too. He just shrugs and says that somebody needed a day off or somebody had a family issue or whatever. He's here, and that's the difference."

"That's true," Spencer said. "Yet sometimes they should probably have more of a life of their own."

"And I think, as long as they're happy doing what they're doing," she stated, "it should be fine. I mean, I'm a prime example. I got up and went to work on my day off," she quipped, laughing at herself.

He grinned. "And that's just somebody who loves their job."

"Or somebody who's an idiot," she replied, chuckling even more. And, with that, the two of them settled in to eat.

BY LATE AFTERNOON Spencer was alone and bored and tired of being in his bed. He thought about trying to get out, but that would mean calling for somebody, and he didn't want to do that either. When a nurse popped around to check on him, he groaned. "I'm fine, you guys. I don't need babysitting."

"Good, I'll put that down." And, with that, she was gone again.

He didn't know if she meant it or whether it would get him off the hook or not. The only thing he'd been able to think about all day was his laptop and the anticipation of food. So he'd emailed Timothy several times. His buddy was pretty excited about coming over to Hathaway House finally. Spencer admitted what he'd done, and it had been a pretty hard and fast conversation, but he was okay about it all now, just feeling a little stupid.

Not everybody who's here wiped themselves out with a simple fall. But he understood the staff's overabundance of caution. Not to mention insurance and all the rest of that liability stuff. He couldn't imagine the headaches involved in running Hathaway House.

When there was no sign of Bella again at dinnertime, he shrugged and waited, wondering whether somebody would call him or if he was supposed to do something about getting food on his own. And then finally deciding that enough was enough, he got into his wheelchair and slowly made his way to the dining room. He knew that, if anybody saw him, he'd probably get in trouble. Yet he could only do so much sitting around and doing absolutely nothing. And, sure enough, Shane saw him first.

He looked at him and shook his head. "Couldn't make it, huh?"

"Nope. Bed rest is just plain torture."

"And yet you spent a lot of time in bed already."

"Exactly, that's why it is so much torture. I came to see if there was any food." He looked around at the line at the buffet. "Apparently my timing sucks."

"No, it's not bad, and it'll move quickly." Shane suggested, "Either you can wait until it clears or you can step into line."

"I can roll into line," he corrected, laughing. "I don't think I can step into it." As he approached, several of the staff stepped back and motioned for him to go ahead. He didn't know whether they did it because of his fall or they were just nice people. He hesitated, and Shane came up and moved him firmly farther into place.

"You're fine," Shane stated. "We always have an eye out for who needs to move forward faster."

"And you know I'm fine too," he protested. Almost immediately Dennis popped up on the other side of the counter, and his big grin had Spencer laughing. "How can you always be so happy?" he asked Dennis in amazement.

Dennis looked at him in surprise. "Why not? Why is it a case of I only get to be happy a few days of the week?"

"I don't know, but I've never met anybody who seemed to have it together quite so much as you do."

"In that case, I need to lose it a time or two, just so you know I'm human." And Dennis waggled his eyebrows and asked, "So what do you want to eat?"

"What's good?" he asked instantly, surveying what was here.

"Everything," Dennis replied immediately.

"It'd better be, otherwise there are problems here." He chuckled. "If that is stir-fry, I'll have some of that."

"It is. Do you want some extra meat?"

And before long he had himself a decent-size plateful.

Somebody else came along, snagged the tray from his hand, and said, "Come on. I'll take you out to the deck."

Surprised, Spencer followed along to find himself firmly ensconced at a table, already half full. Within minutes, it filled up with other people. He didn't know 90 percent of them, but the conversation was amiable, and basically Spencer was so happy to be outside. He had yet to meet a lot of the patients, and this certainly gave him a chance to. He kept looking around to see where Bella was, but, of course, she was on her own time frame and didn't need to be anywhere around here.

By the time his plate was empty, Spencer felt more fatigue setting in, which he had refused to acknowledge earlier. It never failed to amaze him just how quickly he had energy, only then to have it yanked away. You had it, and now you lost it. Didn't make a whole lot of sense, but he had to deal with it regardless. He started to pull away from the table and then saw one of the guys had returned with a massive slice of tiered cake. Spencer pointed at it. "Where did you get that from?"

The guy laughed. "Dennis is handing it out over on the side there."

And, sure enough, Spencer eyed Dennis at a large table, with a massive cake in front of him. He called over to Dennis. "Do you want to save me a piece? I'm coming, I promise."

"Don't bother," Dennis replied. "I'm coming to you."

When he did arrive, Spencer asked him, "How will I ever improve, if you guys keep doing everything for me?"

Dennis nodded. "That's a good point. After this, I guess you get to look after yourself." And, with that, Dennis disappeared.

The guys at the table laughed at Spencer. "Now you're in for it," they said, still laughing. "You'll be sorry you did that."

Spencer asked, "Is it that bad?"

"It's not that bad. It's that good," one guy suggested. "When you make a push for independence, then independence is yours, whether you truly wanted it or not."

"Right," Spencer noted. "I wanted the cake, but I wasn't expecting him to deliver. Yet I should, since he always does."

"It's all good," his dinner companions noted in unison.

"You'll just see how different life can be over the next few days. They really care here, and you'll find that what you thought was independence is a whole lot different than what they thought was simply kindness."

And Spencer was about to find out. He spent the rest of his weekend, calm and quiet. On Monday, he came for his own breakfast. Basically by Wednesday, he was proud of the steps he'd taken at being as independent as possible. By the time Wednesday night rolled around, Bella popped in. He was surprised but feeling quite different.

She grinned at him. "According to the gossip, you have gained some independence."

"What is that?" he asked. "Some kind of a joke around this place?" Yet he flashed her a big grin.

"No, I think it's more of a milestone." She smiled back at him.

"In that case, I'm glad to have it happen," he stated, "particularly since my friend's arriving tomorrow."

She looked at him in surprise and then nodded. "I can't believe how quickly time's going by. It's been a brutal week for me."

"I haven't seen you, so I assumed you were crazy busy. Or you were ignoring me," he teased, again with a big grin.

"Never. Just a crazy-busy week."

He held up a hand. "Believe me. I get it. Everybody's been taking it easy on me in my sessions, so that I'm not too dizzy and not too worn out at the end of them."

"Oh, that makes sense," she noted. "I never even contemplated that, but I can see that they might think that contributed to your fall."

"And they'd be wrong," he said, his lips twisting in a wry smile.

"I came to ask if you were up for a swim," she shared.

He hesitated. "I wasn't planning on it." But he thought about it and nodded. "You know, I'd love to." Not only would he love to go in the water, but he'd love to spend time with her. It had been a disappointment to not see her all week. "I was about to send you an SOS and wondered if you were avoiding me," he said lightly, searching her features.

She looked at him in surprise and shook her head. "Nope, absolutely not. It's just been a rough week for me. I've had one of my guys down and then another one quit," she said, "so I just haven't had two seconds. Working overtime and crashing early."

"Ouch." He stared at her. "And, of course, you've been overdoing it physically because of that."

"Sure have. That's another reason for the swim. I need it," she murmured. "Pretty rough out there."

"Good," he said. "Meet you there in five?" She hesitated, and he realized that last time they arranged to meet was when he fell. "I promise that I won't fall this time."

She burst out laughing. "Then it's probably safe to leave you to your own devices. After all, everybody else has." And, with that, still chuckling, she left.

And he managed to turn around and to change his schedule, so he could have a swim. He couldn't imagine anybody saying no. Bella was a very special person, and he was enjoying every minute with her. A huge break from the regular boredom of this place. He hadn't realized just how much he was looking forward to Timothy's arrival, until he got closer to the date, and now it's all he could think about. But first? ... First was this evening. And that would be special too.

Chapter 10

BELLA FLOATED IN the pool, trying to let her body ease up on some of her own pain, as Spencer wheeled his way toward her. She lifted a hand, so that he knew she was already in the water, and then she started doing laps. When she lifted her head, she saw him beside her, moving slowly but still strong.

After her laps she popped up to the surface, and he popped up, again beside her. She chuckled. "You're a strong swimmer," she noted. "That's got to be a relief, after everything you've been through."

"Absolutely. Yet sometimes, just because you're a strong swimmer, it doesn't mean that, after an accident, you're still a strong swimmer," he replied. "I was afraid I would lose that."

"I'm glad you didn't," she said, with a bright smile. "I'm going to hit the hot tub and soak some of my muscles."

"I'm coming right behind you."

And she deliberately walked away, not knowing whether he needed help or not, but hoping that he could get there on his own. And when he arrived with a look of triumph on his face, she realized just how important his independence was. "I never even think about those things," she muttered.

"What things?" he asked.

"Just how hard it is to get from even the pool to here,"

she noted, "when you're not as able-bodied as you want to be."

"As able-bodied as you want to be," he repeated, rolling that around, and she was afraid she'd insulted him. But then he nodded. "I like that. It puts it in a good perspective. Because," he explained, "there will always be times in everybody's lives when they're not as able-bodied as they want to be."

"I know," she agreed. "Sometimes I overdo it at work, and I'm in the same boat. Yet I don't really think about it because, when you're healthy, you bounce back or expect your body to carry on."

"And it's the expectation that we're supposed to bounce back that hurts," he replied quietly. "Everything else is just something we're supposed to do, but we don't worry about it, until there's a reason, and then that reason is what sidelines us."

"You're right," she stated, "and I know better, but that doesn't stop me."

He chuckled. "That just makes you human, not a fool. Everybody here is dealing with the same thing. I mean, we overdo it in therapy all the time. Partly because we know what we used to do, and, when we get to a certain point in this process, we think, *Of course I can do that.* I mean, I've always been able to do that, except now I can no longer do the same thing. So it's, … it's a fascinating stage."

"I'm glad you have taken it all with such good grace," she murmured. "I'm not sure I would do it half as nicely."

"I think you'd be surprised," he noted. "We never know what we're capable of until life dumps us into the pits, and we're forced to deal with whatever it hands out."

"And, so far, I've been lucky," she said. "Life hasn't been

an easy ride, but it certainly hasn't been one full of strife."

"Then you're blessed. Just count your blessings, and it's all good."

"I wonder if we ever do that though," she murmured, as they wallowed in the hot tub. "Do we ever see how lucky we really are? I mean, we say it. I know how lucky I am, but do I fully appreciate that? I'm not sure."

"I'm not sure either," he replied, looking at her in surprise, "but you're right. We use those words but not necessarily with any intent. We say them, but do we mean them?"

"Exactly. I think most of us know that words are easy and not necessarily connected to deeds."

"Whereas I've learned that words have as much power as deeds," he shared thoughtfully. "And I hope that, going forward in life, I'll have a much better idea of what I'm asking of myself and of others."

"And I think just having that self-awareness is huge," she murmured. "None of us are perfect, and we're all on whatever this journey leads us to called life."

He chuckled. "Now you're starting to sound like Dennis again."

"And that's not an insult," she noted, smiling. "That man? He's a good man, full of heart."

"He is, indeed," Spencer agreed. "And, right about now, I know it's too early for dinner but, wow, I would not be against one of those huge ice cream cones he hands out."

"Does he hand out ice cream?" She lifted her head and looked at him in astonishment. "How is it I don't know about that?"

"I'm not sure." He shrugged. "It's not all the time by any means. But it's just enough times that I know that they're available."

"Wow, I'm feeling very cheated right now."

He burst out laughing. "If we both weren't soaking wet, I'd say one of us should go figure out how to get one of them. But, as it is, that won't happen."

Then Dennis's voice popped over the railing. "I heard that. If you don't pass it around, I'll bring you each one."

Immediately she cheered. "I've never had one, so make mine big. I've been missing out." With that, Dennis disappeared over the corner of the railing. She looked at Spencer and admitted, "I might have just done myself in."

"You might have," he agreed, "but I will sit here in awe and watch while you manage to get your way through one of his concoctions."

"Particularly when I haven't seen them before," she added. "I'm a little worried about that."

"You should be worried," he teased, noting her expression. "You have no idea what's coming."

And when Dennis approached them about ten minutes later, and she took a look at what was in his hand, she gasped and then burst out in laughter. "Oh my God, there'll never be a day where I can eat that." Three tiers high and topped with a cherry. But she reached up with both hands and said, "Gimme, gimme, gimme."

Laughing, Dennis handed them over.

Spencer decided if Bella could ever teach him something, it would be living in the moment and enjoying it. Watching her devour that ice cream, almost to the point of making herself sick, before finally holding up her hands in surrender and saying, "I did what I could, but it beat me."

He cheerfully finished hers and his. Yet she had had such joy in every bite, such emotion and pleasure with everything that she did, and did so openly about it all, that her reactions were the biggest thing that surprised him in this. He'd thought he was somebody who lived in the moment. However, since the accident, he'd always been living in the future—trying hard to get to some point, to hit a goal, to get better, so that something then could happen—instead of living as Bella was.

Yet she wasn't dealing with the same issues he was.

And how much of that was an excuse on his part? How much of that was so he didn't have to think about living more in the moment? All the time he was going through the surgeries, his thoughts were always about how things would get better after the next surgery, things would get better after the next set of rehab, or things would look different after he saw the next doctor.

He had spent his entire life waiting.

Even when Timothy had mentioned this place, all Spencer could think about was that it would be better and that his life would start then. And here he was now, and he was already looking at when things would change and when things would get better. But instead his attitude needed to shift now so that when he physically reached that "better" point in time, it already was better.

A sobering realization. He had never thought that was an issue for him. But, as he was quickly learning, he had things to learn everywhere, around every corner, and with every person, whether he was up for seeing the lessons or not.

When he was away from Bella, his mind kept going in her direction, wondering just what she was up to. Yet he always did so with a smile on his face because he knew that, whatever she was doing, she was doing it at 100 percent—as compared to his doing a lot of his life at just 50 percent. Sure he was working hard with Shane at 100 percent, and, in all honesty, Spencer was also working hard with the shrink at 100 percent, or at least almost 100 percent, or as much as he knew he could handle right now.

The mind-set was the stuff that you thought you were doing well, and then it came up behind you and choked you, until you couldn't breathe anymore. And you hoped that you had enough strength to make it through whatever was coming at you next because so much change was happening, and you could do only so much.

But he felt good about his commitments here; he felt good about his efforts, and that was important. A very sobering thought but, at the same time, also enlivening because it allowed him a different perspective—to see what he could do differently, what he should be doing differently, and potentially take some of that advice for himself and actually do it differently. Because it was one thing to know that you shouldn't be doing something or that you weren't putting in the effort that you should be, but it was another thing entirely to change and to make it something that you could do. Daily. Relentlessly. And that was where he was at right now.

THURSDAY HAD FINALLY arrived, and Spencer was waiting for Timothy's arrival. Timothy had sent texts on a regular basis throughout today, letting Spencer know his progress. And he was out even now in the front waiting room, having canceled everything on his appointment calendar, just so he could be here for his buddy.

When Shane came over with a raised eyebrow, Spencer

explained. Shane immediately nodded. "Good. Should be interesting to meet him."

"He's a character," Spencer noted, with a rueful smile, "but not so great on the self-confidence."

"And yet he told you about this place?"

"He pushed to come here," Spencer stated. "He had a few more issues before the doctors would let him come."

"Yeah, that can hang up a lot of our patients," Shane murmured.

Just then came a commotion at the front door, and a wheelchair was pushed in.

Spencer took one look at Timothy's face and winced. His trip had obviously not been nice or easy. Spencer rolled over and gave his friend a gentle hug.

Timothy murmured, "You're absolutely a golden sight for sore eyes right now."

"Sorry, bud. Seems your trip was pretty brutal."

"That is not the word for it," he muttered. "There is brutal, and then there's this." He was shaking, as he stared up at his friend, his eyes wells of pain.

"Did you take your pain meds?"

"Apparently they didn't come with me. I'm hoping somebody can help me out now that we're here."

"They can," he replied immediately, "but I don't know that they'll do it first off."

Timothy winced at that. "Of course not. There'll be multitudes of testing, et cetera."

"And yet," Spencer noted quietly, "they know all your problems well ahead of time, and I'm sure that they'll be right here to give you a hand."

"And you got my back on this, right? If they don't show up and if you don't see me again, you'll do a full investigation into what happened, right?"

Spencer burst out laughing. "It's not that bad. Remember. This is where you wanted to come."

"Yeah, I kept trying to remind myself about that during the whole trip," he shared.

The pain was still so evident in his buddy's voice that Spencer was happy to see Shane join them, probably giving the two friends a moment or two to talk first. Spencer rolled back and said, "I'll let Shane handle this and get to your room. As soon as I know that you're settled in, I'll come visit you. Yet it might not be until tomorrow morning, considering how late it is already today."

"But it's only noon," Timothy protested.

"And maybe, when you hit your bed, you'll crash."

"Check on me later, if you can."

"I will tonight, even if you are asleep," Spencer promised, and he headed back toward his room. He did have another appointment with the shrink this afternoon, and he wasn't ready to cancel that one. Apparently he had some things to work out. As much as it wasn't the type of sessions he wanted, as long as they worked, he was there for them.

As he walked in, Dr. Minaj looked up at him and smiled. "I hear from the rumor mill that you have a friend arriving today."

"He's here," Spencer confirmed, with a smile. "A little worse for wear but he's here."

"Sometimes the transport is jarring," she murmured. "It'd be nice to think everybody could have a journey that's uneventful. Yet it doesn't happen very often. I'm glad to see you're here with such good spirits. Now we'll park Timothy's problems, and let's deal with yours."

Spencer winced at that but nodded and buckled in to get the work done.

Chapter 11

SO SILLY FOR her to be worried about the arrival of his friend. Yet Bella knew how much Spencer had been looking forward to Timothy's arrival, and she also knew that plans didn't always go the way that you wanted them to. Also quite possibly Timothy's arrival would be less than a success. She had heard how the mere transit was painful. And these rehab patients were most likely already in pain. She wouldn't wish that on anybody, but it happened.

Considering that Spencer had been waiting and waiting for this moment, she would rather that Spencer just forgot about the arrival and didn't get his hopes up. So, when it happened, it would be a great surprise, and, if it didn't happen once again, he wouldn't be stuck in limbo. She fought hard to get those messages across without sounding pushy, something she never wanted Spencer to feel with her.

Still, when she heard from Dennis that Timothy had arrived, she beamed. "I know Spencer was counting on that, so I'm glad to hear he made it to Hathaway House."

"Apparently he had a rough trip."

She grimaced. "I'm not sure that anybody has an easy trip. Seems most have rough trips."

Dennis nodded. "In more ways than one, you're right. So many things can go wrong."

"The transport trips are the worst, especially if they're

coming from a long way away."

"It'll be interesting to see how he handles this."

She looked over at him sideways. "How Spencer handles Timothy, or how Timothy handles being here?"

"Both," Dennis confirmed. "As soon as you add one more face, one more person, the dynamic changes."

"I hadn't thought about that," she noted, "but you're right. It does. The question is whether it changes things for the better or not."

"Exactly," Dennis replied cheerfully. "We're pros at making it work, no matter what."

She smiled at that because, of all the things that Dennis was, he was a cheerleader and had a firm belief in everything that everybody here could do to fix everything potentially wrong around the world. "It's good for Spencer. I know he was feeling bad that he got in before his friend."

"I'm sure there was a reason for that," Dennis noted.

She nodded. "Yet Spencer still felt guilty."

"And guilt is one of those emotions that creeps in and just chokes us," Dennis replied. "So hopefully Spencer can get rid of that, and maybe it won't inhibit him."

"I don't think very much is inhibiting him right now," she said, with a chuckle. "He seems to be going pretty strong on his forward path."

"And I'd agree with that. His progress has been pretty solid. Wonder what his plans are when he's done here?"

She winced. "It's early still, so I have avoided asking too much about that."

He chuckled. "Nothing like avoiding bad news."

"And I don't know whether it's bad news or just no news," she corrected. "He has mentioned that he needs to do some soul-searching, but I'm not exactly sure what that will mean."

"And whether he'll stay locally or not."

She nodded. "I hope so. I want to stay in touch," she admitted honestly.

"You might want to tell him that," Dennis suggested. "Particularly sooner rather than later."

BELLA TOOK DENNIS'S advice to heart and thought about it for the next few days. She was giving Spencer a little break, while he spent one-on-one time with Timothy. She didn't want to intrude, and even that thought was a foreign concept because she wouldn't ordinarily do that. And then she thought about what Dennis had mentioned, about adding one more person to a relationship could change the dynamics. If she allowed it, it would change their dynamics totally.

Yet, then again, if she didn't allow it, she still was a part of however the dynamic changed, just through her inaction. On that note, when her workday ended, she walked to Spencer's room and popped her head in. He was sitting on the side of the bed, looking for the world as if he'd just lost his best friend.

She immediately jumped in. "Are you okay?" she asked anxiously.

He gave her slow nod. "Yeah, I'm okay, but Timothy has gone back to the hospital."

"Oh no," she gasped. "What happened?"

"One of the test results came up with bad news. So they're taking him into the city for more tests. One of the local doctors is taking him on, and he'll be at the hospital there for a while."

"Oh, no," she murmured, "I am so sorry." She was devastated for both of them. Spencer looked around, a little lost. She suggested, "Do you want to do something right now, taking your mind off of it?" He just stared at her, as if not quite sure what to even say or what she even meant because his focus wasn't on her words. "Come on. Let's get to the pool. You can work out some of this in the water."

He looked at her. "I was, … I was hoping to show Timothy the pool."

"And you can," she agreed, hating to hear the desolation in his voice, "as soon as he's back."

"But what if I caused this?" he asked.

She frowned, walked forward, grabbed one of his hands, and held it with both of hers. "Think about what you just said," she urged. "He's the one who wanted to come here. Yes, you got here first, and I know that doesn't sit well with you. However, now he's here, and whatever they found with the first round of testing does not mean it's that bad. It could be something minor."

He raised his gaze to her and asked, "Would they take him to the hospital for something minor?"

"It could be a good sign that they caught whatever when they did. It could be all kinds of things," she said. "He might have had a reaction to one of the medications he was given here. It could be anything. I can ask, but I can't guarantee that anybody'll tell me."

"Timothy would tell me, but then they whisked him away."

"And that's probably the best thing for him," she added. "As long as that doorway is open, he will come through it as soon as he can."

Spencer smiled, rubbed his face with his free hand, and

replied, "You're right, and I know that. Waiting is just frustrating. It took forever for him to get here. Then he's here for a couple days, and, all of a sudden, he's gone again."

"Just remember," she murmured. "He made it here. He's in capable hands, even at some other healthcare facility, and you don't know that it's anything serious."

"No, I don't, and I, … honestly I didn't get a chance to ask anybody."

At that, Shane popped his head into the door, happy to see the two of them here. "I just wanted to give you an update on Timothy. And he specifically told me to tell you, Spencer, and your lady friend."

Spencer lit up. "What's going on?" he asked.

"They found a shadow on one of the X-rays here, so they're sending him in to get a better X-ray done in town at the cancer clinic."

"Cancer?" Spencer repeated.

"They found a shadow on his lung," Shane explained. "That's all we know. It could be just a bad image."

"He had lung injuries," Spencer noted immediately. "And I know that was a bit of a concern way back when because there's scar tissue."

"And that scar tissue could be all it is, but everybody here needs to know ahead of time, before we start working with him."

"Of course you do." Spencer took a deep breath. "If that's all it is," he added, "then that's as minor as I could hope."

"I'm glad you think that way," Shane noted, "because, if you think it's minor, and if you know Timothy as well as you do, then chances are none of us should worry about this repeat event."

"I guess losing people still happens here though, doesn't it?" Spencer asked, looking around.

"Unfortunately it can happen at any time," Shane confirmed, "whether it's here or somewhere else."

"His lungs were a problem before. And there was quite a scare about it. Everybody was being ultra-cautious," Spencer added. "So, if that's what is going on here too, then I'm quite happy for the moment to relax about it all and to believe that this is probably the same issue."

"And that works for me too," she murmured. "That's a perfect answer."

"I don't know about an answer," Spencer corrected, "but I do feel better."

As she studied his face, she realized he looked it too. "So, pool now?"

He looked over at Shane and then nodded. "That's probably a good idea."

Shane nodded. "You do that. It's been a stressful day, and you don't want to keep that stress in your system."

"Maybe not," he murmured. He looked over at her. "Ten minutes?"

"Sure, ten minutes," she said. And, with that, she left to get changed. As she walked over to her place, she thought about how much Spencer had already lost. His parents almost at birth, a loving childhood, his friends from the military, his lifestyle, his military career, and then the thought of losing Timothy and the panic that Spencer must have felt. A swim would be good for him. There was nothing, nothing like the thought of losing somebody you cared about.

And, in this case, she knew that everyone's lives were all intertwined and always held that possibility of death or injury, especially for those with existing injuries or conditions. Just because of the nature of their injuries, not everybody survived the surgeries, not everybody survived for very long after these traumatic injuries. They did the best they could, and they tried hard to do as much as they could for as long as they could. However, when their beaten-up bodies were done, they were done. And that had to be hard for Spencer too. She thought about that, as she now changed and dressed and headed to the pool. She wasn't at all surprised to find Shane pushing Spencer there.

As he jumped into the water, she walked over to Shane and asked, "Has he lost somebody recently?"

Shane frowned, then stared at him. "That's a good question. Timothy's setback hit him hard, didn't it?"

"It did," she murmured. "I just wondered if something was going on here that I didn't know about."

"Chances are, something else is going on," Shane stated. "These military guys didn't come to these injuries easily and rarely alone. Almost always a loss is involved."

She sighed. "It's just more punishment, when they've already been through so much." She sighed. "It's hardly fair."

"And remember..."

"I know. I know." She held up her hand. "Nothing's fair in life."

"No, it isn't," Shane agreed, with a gentle smile. "Are you going in?"

"I so am." She jumped into the water, out of the way of Spencer, smiling as the water closed over her head. If nothing else, she needed this too.

SEVERAL DAYS LATER, still feeling that edginess inside, Spencer heard Timothy would be returning. Spencer felt the pain and the relief wash through him. Tears were in his eyes when Dani told him. He whispered, "Thank you."

And she turned and left him quickly, so that he could get his own emotions under control. He appreciated that. Ever since the accident, Spencer's emotions were all over the place. It had been brought up a couple times by the staff, as if everybody were waiting for the news about Timothy, before dealing with Spencer's reactions to date.

Spencer knew Timothy would update him regardless, but Spencer needed to express these emotions and needed to determine where they were coming from too, as his reactions had been more than normal. Or maybe not. Maybe that's just him. Maybe he was just an emotional guy.

He didn't know what the answer was, but he was hoping that Timothy would be back soon, and they could finally get on with their own scenarios as to future plans and friendship. Spencer would be here for months yet, and he had no idea on Timothy's time frame, but Spencer couldn't imagine it would be less. At least he didn't think so. Still, he was filled with joy when he saw Timothy in his own room again a few days later.

Timothy looked at him, gave him a big grin. "Bet you didn't think you would see me again."

Spencer leaned against the doorjamb, his crutches under his arm because Timothy's room was only a few rooms from his. "I was pretty worried about it."

Timothy's face shadowed. "I won't tell anybody else, but I was too. Every time they do that, my heart just figures *This is it. I'm done.*"

"And we've been through too much already," Spencer

noted. "None of us want to hear anything else going wrong."

"And yet there's always something wrong, isn't there?" He shook his head. "It's a risk in this world."

"Particularly when we're already dealing with so much."

"I know. Sorry for the scare, bud."

"Yeah, you and me both," he said, with a headshake. "Just glad you're back and all is well."

"Yeah, me too," he agreed. "I'm still doing okay, and I'll keep trucking along, as long as I can."

"No particular reason for you or any of us to worry, is there?"

"I don't think so. I mean, doctors are always going on about how you have to take care of yourself, all that *blah-blah-blah* stuff. But they don't seem to realize that we're doing the best we can and that sometimes there's just nothing more we can do."

"I think they realize that part all too well," Spencer noted calmly, "but that isn't our issue now. You're back, and now it's full speed ahead." He motioned at his crutches. "I hope so. I want to walk normally again."

"Hey, you're looking better."

Spencer nodded. "I'm still sitting in the wheelchair most of the time, but I'm straightening up and getting a lot more of my muscles built up, just so I can walk and can get around a whole lot easier."

Timothy smiled, as he studied his friend. "You're looking a lot better."

"Now that I see you, I am," Spencer confirmed. "Just hearing you had to go back to the hospital sent me for a loop."

"And I couldn't have my phone with me for the longest time, so I couldn't give you any updates. That's why I got word to Shane. I didn't want you to worry, but, of course, you worried anyway."

"Of course. We're buds."

"That we are, and I appreciate it. You just have no idea how nice it is to know that somebody out there cares about you."

"I care," Spencer declared. "Now that we're both here together, we can both progress and get better. This place is amazing. The people are awesome, and the animals around the place are a great addition."

"You put any thought into what you'll do when you're done here?" Timothy asked. "You're almost fit enough to get a labor position."

Spencer snorted at that. "Only if I want to end up back in rehab," he stated. "So there won't be any heavy physical work in my world, at least not like that. I mean, gardening maybe, but nothing more than a hobby or some front-yard landscaping."

"I hear you there," Timothy agreed. "You were in strategy and economics. Can you do something along those lines?"

"I don't know. I'm not ready to worry about it. I'll probably have options when I get out of here, but that seems too far in the future to face today. A couple hobbies come to mind, but mostly due to seeing all the animals around. Maybe get back riding again. Maybe learning to make some horse gear." He laughed. "Nothing specific yet, but, hey, I'm leaving things open at the moment to whatever feels like something I'd enjoy. Joy hasn't been a priority in my life since, … well, forever. I aim to change that."

"And yet," Timothy added, "now that I've been given that second chance here, I don't think it's all that hard to sort out. I think it's just you haven't seen enough progress to see what you can do."

"Maybe," Spencer muttered, wondering about that. "See? I told you how it was good to have you around."

He burst out laughing. "And I'm hungry. Do you think we could possibly make our way to the food?"

"I think so. It is almost dinnertime."

"Yeah, I'm not sure I can handle the wheelchair on my own though," Timothy muttered. "And, of course, Shane and Dani already read me the riot act about trying to do too much."

At that, Spencer nodded. "We can probably get somebody to take you there." Timothy wouldn't ask for help. That was for sure. "Sometimes the help comes when you least expect it," Spencer said with a laugh.

"If an angel would come around," Timothy added, "I could use one."

At that, a woman popped her head around the door. "I heard something about an angel. What do you need?"

And they looked over to see this tall, slim, svelte-looking woman in a suit. "Hey, not an issue," Timothy replied. "We'll be fine."

She frowned at him. "What? So I'm not good enough to help you?" she teased. "Or is it my suit?"

Immediately Timothy protested. "That's not what I meant. I was looking for somebody to help me get to the dining room, but I can call an orderly," he said, as he searched the buttons on his remote.

"I work here too," she added. "I know I'm in a suit, but that's a whole different story. I just came from a conference in town."

He looked over at her. "You work here?"

She smiled and laughed. "I know I don't look it, but yes

I do. I'm one of the doctors," she murmured. She walked up behind him and said, "And dinner is very important." She got behind the wheelchair and immediately turned him toward the door. She stopped, looked over at Spencer, and asked, "Are you coming with us?"

"I am but not on crutches."

"Do you have a wheelchair?" she asked.

"I do, and I can go on my own steam," he said.

"Good. You want to meet us at the dining room or do you want us to wait for you?"

He looked over at Timothy, who had a stunned look on his face. "My door's two down," Spencer offered. "I'll meet you there in my wheelchair." And, with that said, moving as carefully and as smoothly as he could, he booked it for his room, where he quickly switched out the crutches for his wheelchair and wheeled from his room. They were already outside in the hallway, waiting for him. And Timothy was still protesting.

"Stop protesting," the doc said. "If I had a dollar for every person I've pushed in a wheelchair, I could retire."

"Hopefully you don't," Timothy admitted. "Because, man, I'll need all the help I can get in this next little while."

"Why this next little while?"

"Timothy just came back from the hospital," Spencer replied.

She smiled and nodded. "That happens," she muttered. "I'm not officially back until tomorrow, but I picked up something for one of our patients that I wanted to deliver myself. But, when I got here, they were busy, so I dropped it off and kept on going. I'll see him tomorrow."

Spencer chuckled, remembering Timothy's recent words. "I'm sure they will appreciate it no matter what, as we find the joy of knowing that somebody cares about what happens to us."

She looked at both of them in surprise. "We certainly do here," she stated.

"So you say," Timothy muttered.

She chuckled. "I presume you only just got here."

"I got here, and then I was sent to the hospital."

"And now you're back again," she replied smoothly, "so everything's different from this moment on."

"I hope so."

At that, another woman called out, "Hey, look at that. There's the two of you." Spencer turned to see Bella, walking toward him. She asked, "May I join the party for dinner?" She looked over at the woman beside him. "Hey, it's Dr. Savannah Pointer. How are you doing?"

"I'm doing great. Just got back in."

"And already at work," Bella added, chuckling. "These guys are a handful anyway."

"They sure are," Savannah agreed.

At that, Bella faced Timothy, smiled, and said, "Hi, Timothy. I'm Bella."

Timothy's eyes lit up. "And I might have heard about you, from this guy," he said, with a nod toward Spencer.

She smiled. "Yeah, Spencer and I tend to have a lot of meals together."

At that, the doctor's phone buzzed. She frowned, looked down at, and Bella stepped in. "Hey, I can take this, if you're busy."

She nodded. "Yes, please. Something just came up. So much for days off." And, with that, she disappeared.

Bella looked over at Timothy. "I hope you don't mind."

He looked at her in surprise and then to Spencer. "Is

everybody this helpful?"

Spencer immediately nodded. "Yes, that's what I mean. Don't sweat it. Every time I turn around, somebody's doing something for me. It took me a long time to realize that I should just accept the help."

"And that's because you have such a hard time accepting any help," she noted, chuckling.

He looked at her and frowned. "I'm not that stubborn."

"Yes, you are."

"Am not."

With good-hearted wrangling all the way to the dining room, Timothy raised his nose and said, "Oh my God, that smells like real food.'

"Welcome to Hathaway House and Dennis's domain," Bella announced, with a bright smile, "because here you're guaranteed real food."

Chapter 12

FOR THE NEXT couple days, every time Bella turned around, the two men were together. Such an odd feeling because there'd been, she thought, a bond forming between her and Spencer, but Timothy's arrival seemed to have changed that. She frowned, as she walked into the dining room, her gaze automatically looking for any sign of the two friends.

As she headed to the buffet line and pulled out a tray, she had to admit to feeling off, disgruntled even, and that was foolish because, if something could be done to help Spencer and Timothy feel better about being here and working harder, then everybody needed to make that happen. She looked up and smiled at Dennis.

His eyebrows rose slowly. "You alone?"

She shrugged. "Seems to be that way now," she admitted. "Kind of weird."

"Or it's just a case of getting used to having his friend here?" he asked calmly.

"Probably that too," she murmured.

She accepted lunch and realized that maybe it would be better if she just backed away for a while and waited to see whether Spencer wanted to contact her on his own or not. She didn't want to get in the way, and she certainly didn't want to do anything to impact his and Timothy's healing.

That was constantly reinforced among the staff because healing was the main reason for all of them being here, and she didn't want to be the one to cause any trouble.

As soon as she sat outside on the deck, she realized that she had shifted her own schedule so much in order to spend time with Spencer that, even now, she had no reason to be here this late. Normally she worked early and then left early, so she had lots of spare time on her own. Something she had foregone in the quest to spend more time with Spencer. And maybe that wasn't good. Maybe she had done that for her own sake but shouldn't have. Such an odd feeling to contemplate, as she sat here eating.

When she looked up to see Dani walking toward her, carrying a cup of coffee, Bella smiled. "Hey, stranger," she murmured.

"Hey, you." She looked around and asked, "The Bobbsey twins aren't here yet?"

Bella burst out laughing. "That's a good name for them, but no."

Dani gave her a curious look. "Are you still spending time with him?"

"Not as much," she shared. "Every time I see him, they're together."

"*Together* doesn't necessarily mean you can't join them though," Dani noted curiously.

"Maybe. They seem to need the time together right now."

"And they do," Dani agreed, with a smile, "yet it probably would be better to not leave them alone much longer. Otherwise Spencer will think you're not interested."

She chuckled. "Relationship advice from this place? It's all about matchmaking here."

"It is not *all* about that," Dani teased, then smiled. "We just want everybody happy."

"If happiness were easy," Bella noted, "it wouldn't be so hard, but it's never quite so simple."

"No, it certainly isn't," Dani admitted. "And adding in the physical and mental wounds to be healed here, it's definitely not as easy around this place."

At that, Bella nodded. "Besides, what difference does it make whether I see Spencer or not?" At that, Dani gave her a flat look, and Bella winced. "Ah, does everybody know I'm interested?"

"Of course," Dani declared. "How would they not? You've spent all your time with him."

"Now I'm wondering if I was spending too much time with him," she admitted, "because I don't want to take him away from what he should be doing."

"And that's appreciated," Dani murmured. "He has a lot that he should be working on. Yet that doesn't mean that you should be avoiding him."

"I'm not," she countered immediately. "I was just looking to see if he was here, and I don't want to disturb him if he's already got arrangements."

"I don't know about arrangements," Dani replied, "but I would imagine that Spencer doesn't want Timothy to be alone or that Spencer needs to help his buddy get around some. So it's more a case of checking to see if his friend is available for a meal."

Bella nodded again. "It's all good," she said quietly. She watched as Dani sipped her coffee. "Do you have many problems with that around here?"

Dani didn't even pretend to misunderstand. "No, not a lot of relationship problems. Every once in a while misunderstandings must be clarified," she explained, "because people get hurt feelings, even when there's no intention to hurt their feelings."

"Ah, is that directed at me too?" Bella asked, with a laugh.

Dani shrugged. "You also matter here. So, if there'll be hurt feelings, then it would be nice if it could be rectified before people did get that far." Just then her phone rang. She looked at it and winced. "And that's the end of my coffee break." She bounded to her feet. "Let me know how it goes over the next few days." And, with that, she was gone.

Bella wasn't even sure what she was supposed to let Dani know about because what was there to say? Spencer was enjoying having this friend around. And Bella was just giving them time and space.

BELLA GOT A text the next day from Spencer. And, when she read it, she laughed out loud.

Miss you.

As soon as her work was done, she headed toward his room. Yet again he wasn't there. The trouble was, she didn't know where he was, and, because she didn't work directly with the staff and the patients here, Bella didn't know what his schedule was. And he could have been anywhere. As she wandered the hallways, feeling foolish, she sent him a text, figuring why not? **I'm at your room. Where are you?**

Coming. Five minutes.

Feeling better about that, she leaned against the wall next to his door and waited until he rolled into view. As soon as he did, he grinned.

"There you are," he said. "I wasn't sure whether Timothy had chased you away or not."

She looked at him in surprise. "And here I was trying to give you time to spend with him."

"He's a friend, but he's just a friend," he replied, with an easy laugh.

"He's an important friend," she stated, with a knowing look.

Spencer grinned. "Yep, we've been friends for years," he shared, "but that doesn't mean I don't want to see you."

"I did come by a couple times," she shared, "but you weren't here."

"And I'm on such a schedule right now," he noted, "so that I'm never here, even when I am here."

She glanced at him and asked, "Where are you at right now for a schedule?"

"*Umm.*" He had to stop and think. He rolled over to his iPad, pulled it out, and replied, "There you go. This afternoon has been canceled."

"Has it though?" she asked, with a suspicious note.

He looked at her in surprise and held up his tablet. "See? Canceled." She smiled at that. "You don't think I would lie, do you?" he joked.

"Absolutely, depending on what anybody wants, then everybody is capable of lying."

"Oh, isn't that the truth," he admitted. However, he put a hand over his heart in a mocking motion and vowed, "I would never lie to you."

"Sure you would," she repeated, chuckling. "Particularly if it got you something you wanted."

"And honestly the only thing I want," he began, with a bright smile, "is to spend time with you."

She rolled her eyes at that. "*Uh-huh*. Like I'll believe that."

"Of course you'll believe it," he stated, "because it's true." And, with that, he motioned toward the dining area and asked, "Have you eaten?"

"I had a little bit for breakfast," she replied. "What about you?"

"I had a light brunch with Timothy," he shared, with an eye roll. "I looked for you, but I figured you'd probably been and gone. So can you stomach a little bit more?" he asked. "Or at least come and have coffee with me?"

"I can handle that." She stepped out into the hallway, watching as he slowly made his way toward her. "You're getting pretty good with that thing, aren't you?"

"*Pretty good* is not the same thing as *getting good*," he corrected. "I want to get *very good*."

"I think everything takes time," she murmured.

"Always way more time than we think."

"How's Timothy settling in?" she asked, as they walked toward the dining room.

"I think he's doing fine," Spencer shared, "and, yeah, I did spend a lot of time with him early on. I was pretty worried about him, after the hospital visit," he admitted. "And then I realized that I was spending so much time with him that I hadn't seen you in days." He frowned, looked at her, and stated, "You don't *need* to spend time with me, right?"

A laugh burbled out. "Nope, I never felt I needed to do that."

"Good, I'd hate for you to feel this was more of a duty than anything."

"Nope, I enjoy spending time with you."

He grinned at that, his face looking boyish and young. "Good, that makes me happy too."

She chuckled. "And now that we've got that out of the way …"

"Exactly. I wasn't even sure how much time had gone by, but, in this place, it just seems the days run into each other. I don't have any concept of how many have gone by," he shared. "Then, all of a sudden, I missed seeing your beautiful smile."

She grinned at that. "And what a lovely thing to say," she stated warmly. "I was just trying to give you some space, so that you could enjoy being with your friend."

"I've had enough space," he said bluntly. "I love my friend dearly, but I do want to spend time with you." And on that note, they walked and rolled into the dining room together. She had to admit she was pretty happy with everything he'd shared with her. And she didn't want to make a big thing out of it, but she enjoyed spending time with Spencer and not having Timothy with them. Mostly she figured because she still wasn't exactly sure what Spencer and she meant to each other.

By the time they had their plates full, and they headed toward the deck for lunch, she asked, "Do you spend all your time with him?"

"I did at the beginning, but he's getting into some of the heavy rehab training now," Spencer explained. "I know what that's like. He should be crashing every day pretty early. So I wanted to give him a little bit more space yet again. Whereas, for me, it's more about adapting and having to kick up some of the progress that I've had already, into some new progress. And that's, … that's a bit of a challenge too."

"As long as you're okay," she murmured.

He nodded. "I'm doing just fine, and it's a weird thing to realize just how many people are always looking out to make sure I am okay."

"Is that a problem?"

"No," he replied cautiously, "but, when you disappeared, I wasn't sure if maybe it was on purpose."

She stopped and looked at him. "Wow, obviously I left you alone too long."

"Yep, obviously you did," he confirmed, again with a bright smile. "So if you've got a reason for not being around, then that's fine," he added, "but, if it's because you don't want to spend time with me, that's also fine. Just let me know, so I'm not hanging on."

"We can stop that conversation right there," she stated. "I enjoy spending time with you. And I was missing you too, but I didn't want to interfere."

"Next time interfere," he told her, chuckling. "We can get caught up in our own world, and yet it's not necessarily the world that we want to be in. It just passes the time of day. But believe me, I want to spend as much time with you as possible."

"Good," she replied. As she set down her tray, she asked, "Do you want me to brew a coffee or anything for you?"

"No, I think I'll be just fine here." And he motioned off to the side. "Maybe a little sun though."

They quickly shifted tables, and she realized other people were watching them.

"Seems we've attracted some attention," he murmured calmly.

"Does it bother you?" she asked.

"Me, no, but what about you?"

"Why would it bother me?" she asked in astonishment.

He studied her face for a long moment and smiled. "No reason, just something that Timothy pointed out."

"Ah, and what's that?" she asked, studying his face, looking for a clue as to what was going on.

"Nothing major, just how you say something in passing, and it never occurred to me that maybe you didn't want to be seen with me."

She stared at him, as she sat with a hard *thunk*. "Have I ever given you that impression before?"

"No, that's why it never occurred to me. Just something that Timothy noted in passing about people that he knew who no longer wanted to be around him."

"I'm sorry for Timothy's sake," she replied. "A lot of people can be that way, mostly because they're unsure how to react when it comes to a physical disability. Whereas this is all I've ever known of you. So I have no reason to be uncomfortable."

At that, he chuckled. "Good point," he murmured. "I hadn't considered it from that point of view."

"And life is way too short for all that miscommunication. Just ask me. And I'll tell you."

"And misunderstandings are always at the root of things, aren't they?" he asked sadly. "Because ... Timothy had experienced that."

"I think a lot of people who are in wheelchairs or with other disabilities have similar experiences," she said. "You just have to, I guess, ignore all that noise, get up, and keep going. However, even without the wheelchair, I've had major miscommunications, so we all need to do our best to keep the lines of communication open—honest and clear communication." She looked at the salad in front of her and smiled. "They do make a mean salad here."

"I don't even know how you can survive on salad." Spencer pointed to his protein-heavy plateful.

"I don't survive on it," she protested, "but I do enjoy it."

"And I get that," he murmured. "Still, it's not enough food for me."

"Not for me either, and I might get something more afterward," she added. "So glad that there aren't any food rules or regulations here, and I can go back and get what I need when I need it," she murmured.

"Oh, that's a good point too," Spencer agreed. "I guess I didn't have to take all this at once."

"Considering how quickly the food here disappears, I wouldn't wait too long," she suggested. "Chances are you'll lose out on a selection, if nothing else."

He winced at that. "And that's another good point." He chuckled. "Just, … just so we're clear, I do enjoy spending time with you."

She smiled, reached across the table, and laced her fingers with his. "And I'm glad to hear that because I do too."

SPENCER WASN'T SURE where his insecurity came from, but, after a number of days where he'd worried about whether she was avoiding him or not, finally Timothy told Spencer that he should just reach out and contact her, instead of twisting himself up into this pretzel of emotions, only to find out that she'd been giving him space.

But it wasn't space he wanted. He wanted time with her. While good to see Timothy, Spencer didn't want to spend all his time with him. Yes, Timothy was going through his own stuff, and Spencer would be supportive. However, at the same time, Spencer had his own stuff to go through too.

As the days that followed grew into a pattern, where he spent some of his meals with Timothy and some with Bella, Spencer felt some of his confidence returning. When he finally said something to Shane about it, Shane stared at him in surprise.

"That's interesting for you to have a confidence issue," Shane noted, "because, in many ways, that wouldn't bother a lot of people."

"I just wanted to make sure she was spending time with me because she wanted to," he shared quietly.

"And the fact that you even contemplated that she wasn't is also surprising."

"I didn't, until just after Timothy's arrival and something he mentioned."

"Ah, nothing like a friend's perspective to change your outlook."

"And I know it's wrong," Spencer murmured. "And I didn't have any reason to misunderstand that she wanted to spend time with me or not, yet it just felt odd."

"I'm glad you brought it up with her then."

"I'm glad I did too, and now I'm spending time with both of them. Sometimes it works, and sometimes it doesn't."

"And does it work to put them together?"

"Not at the moment," he admitted. "And I think that's mostly on me. I'm jealous of the time I get to spend with her."

Shane grinned. "And that's a good thing, and good also that you'll fight for what's important for you."

He stopped and stared at Shane, perplexed. "Have I given you the impression that I'm not?"

"Not necessarily, but, when you have friends here, your priorities can get twisted a little bit," he explained. "And the important thing is to realize that your priority needs to be you, always needs to be you," Shane declared, with that same calm attitude that Spencer had become used to.

"And I always thought it was," Spencer replied. "So it's interesting that you see it differently."

"I think it is. I think it's also just a case of your not wanting to upset anybody. Like your friend."

"No, of course not. Which makes me sound foolish, doesn't it?"

"No, not at all. If you want to spend more time with other people, you just need to make that clear."

"I don't think Timothy is putting any demands on me," Spencer noted. "If anything, I'm the one probably putting the demands on me."

"Ask him then. Maybe next time you're with him, ask him if he needs more space. And, if you don't think he does or if you think your friend will claim you're an idiot for even asking, then don't worry about it."

He chuckled at that. "That's good advice."

"Communication is usually just about opening up the doors and letting people say what they need to say," Shane noted, with that same confidence. "So just let it happen. And, if you care about her and if you want to spend time with her and if you think it's a relationship that's developing into something durable over time, then your friend will understand."

"I guess I never explained it to him," Spencer admitted. "That's my fault."

"And it doesn't mean that fault is involved," Shane corrected. "View it as pointing out that clarification is needed."

Sure enough, when he brought it up with Timothy a few days later, Timothy looked at him as if he were nuts. "Good Lord," he said. "You have a chance to spend time with a beautiful woman, so don't choose me over that." Timothy laughed out loud. "And I'm not much good company right now. I appreciate that you were here for me when I first arrived, but it's gotten down to serious business now. So I don't always have the *oomph* to get up and to care about anything else."

"You're not supposed to," Spencer agreed, recognizing his friend and where he was at. "I remember those days. Some days I relive those earlier days. We have enough to do on a daily basis that you always must look after you first and foremost."

"And that's what I was trying to do," Timothy stated. "So, if you get a chance to spend time with her, please do."

THE NEXT DAY, feeling better about that and hating that he felt he was cheating his friend in the first place, Spencer found himself with an early end to his day and contacted Bella. **Pool time?**

Absolutely. Do you want to invite Timothy?

He thought about it, then realized, no, he didn't. He just wanted to go to the pool and to spend time with her. And, with that, he sent back a quick text. **Nope, I'll meet you there in twenty.**

Even getting dressed and making his way there was hard. By the time he was poolside, she was already floating in the water. And it just added to his sadness, and he didn't even know why.

She must have seen something on his face because she immediately pulled herself up and asked, "What's the matter?"

"I don't know, just an off day," he replied, not wanting to get into it. But she wouldn't let him get away with that.

She groaned. "You know, off days have reasons. Maybe you should let me know what the off day's all about."

He nodded. "It's stupid, but, all of a sudden, I was just sad. Timothy is doing much better. I'm doing much better. And the world's changing again."

"In a good way?" she asked.

"Yes, in a good way, which is also why it's stupid that I'm feeling anything negative about it." He shrugged, yet smiled. "Don't worry about me. I'm … just having a weird day."

"I'm glad to hear Timothy is doing better," she said. "It would be hard to watch your friend not necessarily have the same success as you are."

"And I think he'll probably see the same success," Spencer suggested. "Until now, I guess I just hadn't seen how everything was moving forward and how that change needs to happen. I could be gone before he is, and I hadn't considered that either. Yet it makes sense."

"Of course it does," she agreed. "Yet again you've been waiting for your friend to get here for so long that maybe the waiting in itself was something that you were accustomed to but not necessarily enjoying the moment."

"And that was another thing," he shared, looking at her in surprise. "I've found that I've spent so much time waiting for life to happen, and I don't want to do that anymore."

"I agree with that," she said on a nod. "It's easy to do, I think, and yet much harder to remember to live in the moment."

"And still you seem to be pretty good at it," he admitted curiously.

She stared at him in surprise. "I don't know about that, but I have a very physical job, and I focus very much on the work that I have to do. So I'm not sure that my case is necessarily the same, yet I do try hard to spend time just enjoying the day, if nothing else." She shrugged. "There always seems to be so much to do that, if I can't get it done that day, I feel guilty. I, … I just want to do whatever I can to finish it, so that it's off my plate." She shook her head. "Somehow I've gotten to the point now where it's a case of *Don't, it'll take however long it'll take. It'll require whatever it'll require.* So I remind myself that I need to just let it be and to let it happen." She chuckled. "And the evenings are similar. I have a pretty laid-back life here. Sometimes I think I should move on and do something else, but I love being here."

"And you're blessed to be here," he noted. "There are so many good things about living here."

"There are," she murmured. "There are also challenges."

"Oh, I get that." He nodded. In the water he floated, feeling some of the stress from the last few days ease away. "I hadn't even realized that I was getting stressed, and now I can feel the pain easing back."

"And that's good. It'll be a process, I suspect."

"Exactly," he murmured. "Like everything else."

She smiled. "Got it. I think maybe more important is to just celebrate the small things and look forward to the big things, but remember to smile every day and to enjoy the passage of time. Because, before long, your time here will be over, and you'll be heading off to whatever comes next."

Something about the way she said that made his heart jolt. Because, when he left, how would he see her again? And yet they were not even close to having that conversation. Although as friends, they were. "So when I leave," he asked lightly, "will you forget me?"

She looked at him in surprise. "I don't see that ever happening. Have you any idea what you want to do or where you will go?" she asked quietly.

"I've put some thought into it, more questions than anything else," he admitted, with a nod. "So I haven't exactly come up with a solution."

"And maybe that's not part of today's worry either," she noted. "We have so many things in life to worry about, so let's not push for things that we don't have to."

"No, but this feels very much as if it's coming toward me."

"You haven't been here that long," she protested. "I suspect you'll probably still be here for another month or two anyway."

"Absolutely, if not twice that," he murmured. "Yet somehow that passage of time coming toward me will happen faster than I think."

"Sometimes every day seems to be dragging along, and you can't get it to move, and the next day is just another drag, and you can't get anything to move," she murmured. "Then, all of a sudden, every day runs so fast that you can't do anything but sit in amazement, as it disappears on you."

He nodded. "I've just hit that point now suddenly," he murmured. "And you're right. It is this bizarre state. However, it also feels right in some way."

"Good," she replied. "And feeling right is important."

He chuckled. "Back to that cheerleader thing."

"I don't even know what I'm doing, if that's, ... if that's what it is." She gave him a bright smile. "Honestly I'm just trying to be a good friend."

"And, if I never mentioned it before, I'll say it now. You are a good friend, and you've been a hugely influential friend, while I've been here." He needed to say it, but he couldn't get the words out for all the emotions choking his throat.

She reached out a hand. "Ditto. I hate to even hear of you talking about leaving," she admitted, "but I understand that your life can't just be frozen."

"No, it can't," he agreed. "At the same time, I certainly wouldn't want to leave without having some idea where you stand in terms of a relationship with me."

She stared at him in surprise. "Isn't this early for that talk?"

His heart clenched at the thought. "I'm not so sure about that. I have to admit that I'm a bit of a teddy bear, and, if we're not heading down the same pathway, my heart'll break. I think I'd rather it broke now than later."

"I think we're heading down the same pathway," she replied cautiously, "but obviously we have a few months to go before we both are no longer here at Hathaway and have logistics to work out."

"There are always logistics to work out," he stated, with a nod. "I guess I was just hoping that we were heading in the same direction."

"I want to think we're heading in the same direction," she restated, "but I'm not exactly sure what direction you want to go."

Chapter 13

BELLA SPENT THE next few days trying to figure out what she wanted to do about her future.

When she saw Spencer again, he murmured, "That's a very pensive look on your face."

"Is it?" she asked. "Just lots of thinking about my future."

"Hey, I thought that was my job," he said jokingly.

"It is, and I'm wondering what you're thinking about," she shared. "Here I've been suggesting that you needed to live in the moment and not worry about it, but, at the same time, the future is rushing toward you."

"And now you're starting to sound panicked," he noted. "What brought that on?"

She shrugged. "Our earlier conversation."

"Right, and I've been considering it all since we've had that talk," he admitted. "Particularly when I'm always putting out milestones to reach before doing something in my life. Such as thinking that, when I got back on my feet, then I could have a relationship. When I got back on my feet and bought a house, then I could have a relationship. When I got my career lined up again, then I could have a relationship because I'd have something to offer."

"Not so much consideration in terms of emotional readiness though," she noted, "but more in terms of financial and physical readiness."

He nodded. "And one of the things that you brought up made me stop and maybe smell the roses a little bit and realize that that wasn't an effective way of looking at my future. Maybe I needed to consider what I wanted to do now and to live in the moment now."

"Good for you."

"Having Timothy here is another example. I kept waiting and waiting for him to arrive, thinking that, when he was here, things would get better."

"Were they bad before?"

"No, not at all," he replied. "I just thought they would get better because he was here. Instead I should have been thinking about how great they were regardless of whenever Timothy got here."

"I think it's a rut that is easy to fall into," she murmured. "And I'm not even sure that you can look at it as being in a rut. I mean, it's just almost a habit," she said helplessly. "I don't even know what else to call it."

"I think that's a decent way of looking at it," he agreed. "So why are you all of a sudden worried about your future?" She hesitated. He looked up, frowning at her. "Is it something I said?"

"No, not at all," she replied. "It's just that reminder that not everything is set in stone and not everything will go the way I want, so how long do I want to be here?"

"I thought this is where you wanted to be," he stated, puzzled.

"It is." And then she stopped. "But, if you won't be here, I don't know that I want to stay."

He stared at her, his heart warming. "I think that's the nicest thing anybody's ever said to me."

She looked at him in surprise. "I doubt it," she replied, laughing.

"No, really. I mean, I was worried about it," he admitted. "I am talking about going back into my field, although I might have to take some college classes to upgrade my education—which would be an odd thing to go back to school again. Yet I could do all kinds of things. I just hadn't thought about what I wanted to do because I'm still stuck in that when-I'm-better mode."

"And yet you also know that, even before you're better, you already need something lined up."

"Exactly," he agreed, "so that goes against our *living in the moment* thing."

"I think the lesson is to live in the moment but to prepare for the future maybe." She tilted her head, chuckling.

"Maybe, and sometimes we can get hung up on all that, and it doesn't make any sense, but we still force it into the old status quo mold, as if it's the theme that we're trying to work with."

"Oh, that's interesting too," she noted. "So, if you were to do something along that line, were you looking at going back to California?"

He shook his head. "No, I had been originally wondering about moving to Florida. I do enjoy the climate there."

"Although Texas is pretty darn nice."

"It's not hard to take at all," he replied. "I just didn't have any experience with Texas up until now."

"Right. And now?" she asked.

"As you said, and we're skirting around the real issue here, but, if I move away, I won't see you," he noted, with half a smile. "And that's not what I want either."

"Good, so at least we've got that much sorted out." She

flashed him a bright grin. "And, if you at least stay local, I can keep this job, and I have to admit that my heart is here."

He nodded. "I can see that, and I don't have a problem with that. We should all be so lucky to have a fantastic job. So, if I stay in town, that would work out as well."

She beamed. "It absolutely would." Then her face fell. "However, it's also important for you to do whatever you feel is right for you."

"Ah, now you've come to let me off the hook again."

She looked up at him in surprise, then shrugged. "Is that what I'm doing?"

He nodded again. "Yep. So many people do that. You make decisions, heading down a pathway, and then you realize that maybe I'm making that decision for somebody else, not for myself. Therefore, probably not the best decision that I could have made, so you back off, letting me change my mind."

She stared at him, and her jaw dropped. "All of that at once? I wouldn't have thought I had that much cognitive awareness of the problem to have done that."

"You probably aren't aware of what you were doing." He chuckled. "But let's get this clear. I do want to see you. I do want to stay in contact, and I want to stay close. While I am footloose and fancy-free, I don't have a visible means of support, outside of my pension, but you do. So it makes much more sense for me to stay local, while I sort myself out."

"A good university is here, several of them," she added hopefully.

"And I haven't even looked into that. I probably would go to school to get some classes."

"Or you could circumvent it." She hesitated and then

brought up her phone. "I admit that I was getting way ahead of myself, but a couple teaching positions are open."

He looked at her in surprise. "At one of the universities?"

She looked up, smiled, and nodded. "Yeah. But, honestly, I'm not the person to talk to about this because I don't know what you have for an education. Yet I found this." And she forwarded him several ads.

He looked at them in surprise. "I was thinking about teaching again. It's a much nicer, slower pace and would allow me to get back into the civilian world, after all this rehab," he explained. "So it's not out of the realm of possibility."

"They are looking for a lot though."

He nodded, as he studied the prereqs. "Nothing I don't have though," he stated. "And, no, you weren't interfering," he added, with a smile.

"I was," she admitted. "I don't want to be pushy, but I was hoping that if you got a local job …"

He grinned. "And I do want a local job, and I do want to see you again."

She beamed. "And that would be nice."

Just then Timothy rolled into his room. He looked around and asked, "Ah, is this a private talk, or can I join in?"

"You're always welcome to join in," she replied. "Besides, I'm heading to get some food. What about you guys?"

Spencer looked over at Timothy. "Do you want to come join us?"

Timothy shook his head. "No, but I was hoping to talk with you for a moment though, if you don't mind."

And just enough anxiousness filled Timothy's voice that she stepped back and said, "I have to go talk to Dani anyway.

Why don't I leave you guys for a bit, and then we'll meet up later?" Not giving them much chance to argue with her, she quickly raced away. It was important that he talk with Timothy as much as Timothy needed. She wasn't sure what was going on in Timothy's world, but he needed Spencer at the moment. She didn't have a real reason to talk to Dani, so Bella just hid in the reception area and then walked around in the front yard, looking at the flowers.

When she got a short text from Spencer, just saying that Timothy had left, she slowly made her way back inside again. She poked her head around the door to Spencer's room and asked, "Are you still up for dinner?"

He frowned. "I'm not sure. ... Timothy has a problem that I don't feel I can share, but I ..." He hesitated.

She nodded. "I understand. We can do dinner tomorrow night."

He looked up in relief. "Would you mind?"

"Of course not. Timothy is a good friend of yours. If he's got some trouble, and he needs your support, absolutely. I'll go have dinner now and maybe head to the pool afterward."

"I might meet you there later too," he offered. "I'm not exactly sure where this will end up tonight."

"If I can do anything to help, let me know," she said, hating to see Spencer twisting in concern for his friend.

He shook his head. "No, we probably just have to do a bit of research on it first."

"Okay, if there is, though, let me know." And, with that, she headed toward the dining room for dinner.

When she stepped in, Dennis looked at her and stated, "You're alone."

"Yep, I am tonight. He needs to help Timothy out with

something."

"Ah, that's a good thing for him to keep his friends."

"Right. I don't want to come in between that," she stated, with a bright smile.

"No. And, in Hathaway House, known for its amazing rehab, maybe Timothy needs a little more than what he's been getting so far."

"I can't imagine that," she said, "but I will take some food. I am hungry." And, with a laden plate, she headed out onto the deck. She sat here, not even alone because very quickly her table filled with other people. She visited with a lot of friends that she hadn't spent much time with because she'd been with Spencer so much.

When one of them brought up Spencer, she replied, "He's with Timothy right now."

They nodded and shared, "Right, something went wrong with Timothy's financial aid, covering his stay here."

She looked at him in surprise. "Seriously?"

"Yeah, it happens sometimes. We have to fight to get the acceptance through sometimes, and they don't always approve it. I know they're all working on it, but I'm sure he's a little disconcerted over the way this has gone."

As she finished her dinner and walked toward her place, she wondered about that. Did everybody just get automatic funding, or was that something that other people decided wasn't needed, and, therefore, they weren't eligible for? It would suck if that were the case. Timothy was already here and was already showing signs of improvement, and she didn't know how anybody could possibly pull that away from him. Yet she didn't want to be anybody who got sucked into gossip at this point, particularly in this case because it would impact Spencer and her relationship with him. But she did think about it a lot later, as she soaked in the pool, yet subconsciously looking for him.

When he didn't show, she realized that she might as well just give up. And she retired to her room for the night.

"THERE HAS TO be some way to get some assistance for you," Spencer said, but they'd both already checked online as much as they could.

"I don't know how," Timothy replied, shaking his head. "This is so messed up."

"How does this even happen?" Spencer asked. "We were both injured in the same on-base training exercise."

"I know. I know. I know. I mean, I get all that," Timothy admitted, "but to think that I'm here, after everything I've been through and getting better, yet to have that being yanked away."

Spencer understood, and his heart bled for his friend. "I suggest you get as much rest as you can, and we'll tackle this again in the morning. I don't think this will be the first time Dani's ever heard of it happening, and maybe she has some solution."

Timothy perked up slightly at that. "Maybe," he said hopefully. "I hate to even bring it up with her. It's so embarrassing."

"I'm sure she already knows," Spencer pointed out. "Anything to do with the budget must go directly to her."

"I know. And that just makes it even more difficult. But …" He slowly wheeled himself to the doorway. "Sorry for screwing up the bigger part of your day."

"Dude, that'll never be an issue," Spencer declared. "Particularly when it comes to this."

"Yeah, I was hoping you didn't mind." He looked at the watch, winced, and added, "We more or less missed dinner."

"And that's okay. I might go get a bowl of soup or something. I wasn't too hungry anyway," Spencer lied.

"Can we still get something?" Timothy asked.

"Sure can. You want to go now?"

Together the two of them slowly made their way to the dining room. As they entered, Dennis looked at them and noted, "Oh, those are long faces."

But neither one was in for talking. They just nodded and asked, "Are there any leftovers?"

"Something is always here," he noted. "You just don't have as many choices."

"I don't think choice is an issue today," Spencer murmured. Shortly Dennis brought out two plates of pork chops and veggies and salad. The men sat in the dining room, without talking, and quickly ate. As soon as dinner was over, they both parted and headed back to their rooms.

As soon as Spencer got to his room, he sat in one depressed mess. He was grateful that it hadn't happened to him. No doubt about that, yet so disturbing to see it happen to somebody who needed an answer, thought that this would be the answer, only to have it yanked out in front of him, which was not fair. Spencer didn't have any money to help, and he didn't know if anybody around here could help his buddy, but Spencer sure hoped so. By the time he got to bed, his dreams were tough and sad.

SPENCER WOKE UP even more depressed, and, by the time

he saw Shane that next morning, Shane looked at him, nodded, and said, "I see the news has hit already."

"Yeah, it sure has. And it's nothing but bad news." The anger inside him needed to be worked out. And Shane was happy to oblige. By the time Spencer's session was done, he was exhausted but still angry. When he left, he turned and looked back at Shane. "Is there any funding for guys like Timothy?"

"Talk to Dani," Shane suggested quietly. "I'm not sure what is available."

And, with that, Spencer had to be happy. He turned and rolled out and headed toward the pool. Not even lunchtime but he was just stressed enough that he knew it would be hard to get anything done today if he didn't go chill somewhat. After a swim, he felt marginally better. And after lunch without Bella, he headed to Dani.

Dani looked up, and he knew from the look on her face that she already knew what he was there for.

"Is there anything you can do?" he pleaded.

"I'm working on it," she replied, a depressed tone to her voice. "I'm sorry. It does happen but not very often."

"No, of course not. You can't run a business like that."

"It's not even a business issue," she noted. "We do take a certain number of charity cases a year, but we're full up right now." He frowned at that. She explained it further. "There can only be so many beds where I do this. Otherwise I can't keep the numbers crunching in the right direction."

He nodded. "Are there any charities that I can apply for on his behalf, anything I can do?"

"And again, I'm looking into it," she repeated quietly. "Give me a day or two."

"And can he stay for that day or two?"

"Oh, absolutely," she stated, with a gentle smile. "And the fact is, he is doing much better here, so we've got an appeal in on his benefits," she murmured. "But these things can take a little bit of time. He gets to stay while that happens."

"And that's good," Spencer noted, "but it's still a noose around his neck."

"It absolutely is," she agreed. "And we know that it's pretty hard to heal—even for you—with all this just sitting here, a rejection waiting to happen. But you have to trust that we're doing everything we can," she stated firmly.

And, with that, he had to be happy.

Chapter 14

WHEN BELLA STEPPED in to see Dani the next day, Dani looked up and asked, "Please don't tell me that you're asking on Timothy's behalf too?"

She winced. "I guess everybody is asking, aren't they?"

"Yep, they sure are, and I get it. But sometimes it doesn't always work out. We've got an appeal in, and I just ... I don't know if there's any more money for him." She sighed. "And staying here is not cheap."

"No, I bet it isn't," she murmured.

"And I do take on several pro bono cases annually, but I can't do it all the time for everyone," Dani murmured. "And, of course, it's even worse because Timothy has been here and has already gone through so much."

"I hear you there. I'd offer a few thousand dollars, but that's all I've got," she admitted, "and that's not even a drop in the bucket."

At that, Dani shook her head. "It's a help, but you're right. It's just a drop in the bucket. It's an incredibly expensive process to be here. I have yet another phone call to make to see if I can get any help," she murmured. "Then I'll talk to a couple of the past patients, who have set up some assistance programs as well. Trouble is, we need a decent amount of money."

"Right," Bella agreed. "Well, if there's anything I can do,

let me know."

"What we can do is keep Spencer on track," she noted calmly. "And I know that's not easy either."

"No, I think he's in danger of going completely off the rails right now," Bella replied.

"So then do what you need to do to help Spencer."

She smiled and nodded. "Right, priorities."

"It's always their priority to do what is best for their own healing," Dani stated, her voice serious and earnest. "It's always about getting them into the best frame of mind, where they can make the best use of everything that we've got here for them. Their healing is everything."

And, with that, Bella had to be happy. Yet a pall hung over Hathaway House, as everybody realized what was going on. Some people were offering up basically pennies in the grand scheme of things, and Bella had offered up a few thousand, but, again, just small change. When she did see Timothy, he was trying hard to smile, but obviously his heart was crushed.

"At least," he said, with a bright smile at her, "Spencer found you here."

"That's true," she replied, with a chuckle. "And I'm very grateful that he's been here, so I got a chance to meet him."

"Yeah, it's just … everybody doesn't always get to win the lottery," Timothy replied.

"Shouldn't need a lottery to get decent health care," she muttered.

"No, it shouldn't, but it sure seems to be sometimes." And, with that, he headed off for another one of his sessions.

She looked over at Spencer, intent on distracting him at least, if not uplifting him. "Hey, you up for a tour around the gardens?"

He looked at her in surprise and then shrugged. "I guess."

"Don't give me faint praise."

He frowned. "I never heard that phrase before."

"It just means, don't be so enthusiastic, when obviously you don't want to go." She shook her head. "We don't have to, maybe going to the pool instead."

"No, I wouldn't mind getting outside for a bit. It is depressing around here right now."

"And a reminder to make the most of every day," she added.

"I've had enough progress that—and I already asked Dani about it—if, … if I left, could Timothy have my spot."

"I don't think it works that way," she noted, "but what a wonderful gift to give to your friend." Bella was touched that he would even think of it.

"That's what Dani said—that it doesn't work that way. At the same time I also know that she can't do anything underhanded to make it happen, but I really, really, really wanted my friend to have the same benefits that I have."

"I totally understand that." She led him past the vet clinic and out to where Hoppers was stretched out in the sun.

"He's got the life, doesn't he?" Spencer asked, looking at the big rabbit.

"He does, but it's also a difficult one," she murmured. "He used to have a lot more freedom, and now he doesn't."

"Ah," he murmured. "I hear you there."

"And it's not always that easy either to give him more space out here, plus keep him safe," she added, "but we try hard." Outside she led Spencer through some of the pathways and completely kept Spencer busy and distracted with the talk about all the work that she'd been doing around here over the last four years.

"You do put your heart into this place, don't you?" he asked in amazement.

"Absolutely, it's very important for me to be here and to see how well everybody is doing and enjoying what I can do for them," she shared.

"And it is a very special place," he murmured.

As they continued to walk, she added, "Sometimes I think things are meant to be and happen for a reason, and then sometimes I think the reasons are completely worthless and just an excuse to deal with ugly things."

"Timothy is handling it better than I would be, if it were me," Spencer admitted. "I'd be kicking and screaming and shouting that I didn't want to go anytime soon and that I'd be doing everything I could to stay."

"I think he is. He's fighting as much as he can, on as many levels as he can, but it's got to be exhausting too," she noted. "And that also slows healing, even your own healing."

He groaned. "I know. I know. I've already got lectures from Shane about it because I'm not functioning as well as I could be."

"And that's to be understood as well," she added. "How many people can function reasonably well when this is happening around them?"

"And yet I should be doing the best that I could because I'm here and I have that opportunity," he replied fiercely, "whereas poor Timothy doesn't."

"I get it, but feeling guilty because you're not enjoying or putting in a 100 percent effort when you're distracted and upset isn't very healthy either."

He hit the arm of his wheelchair. "It's hard to refocus, with so much going on."

"It is, indeed. We can always set up a GoFundMe site for Timothy. And sometimes we have to look at all the negatives that are happening in life to pick up on all the positives," she murmured. She crouched in front of him, reached for his hand, and said, "I know this is a rough time for you and for Timothy, but I still am happy that you came here."

He reached out and touched her cheek gently. "Me too. I never thought to ever have anybody in my life and to feel about her the way I feel about you," he murmured. He tilted her chin and studied her face for a long moment. "I just wish that—"

And then she placed a finger against his lips. "I know. I know. Let's just keep hoping that some solution will happen and that miracles still occur."

"I know they do here," Spencer replied. "I've seen it in my own healing and in others," he murmured. "I just need one more miracle for Timothy."

"And because you're asking for a miracle for somebody else, maybe you'll get it," she said, with a bright easy smile.

"I sure hope so." He looked around, seeing the other animals that had been rescued, and a miracle had happened for them. "Dani has done so much for so many different animals," he noted. "It would be nice if she could find one more bit of help for Timothy."

"You know that, if it's possible, she'll do it," Bella declared. "And we have to let her do whatever she can do."

He nodded. "It's just so hard to wait. And what am I supposed to do in the meantime?"

"You do the best you can. And then, when we find out, whatever the news is, whichever way it'll go, we make the best of it," she declared quietly.

He looked up at her. "When did you get to be so smart?"

She chuckled. "I'm not sure that I am. I'm just happy that, so far, it looks as if life has been a little bit decent. After all, it brought you into my life," she said in a cheeky tone.

At that, he burst out laughing. "You are good for me. If nothing else, you always remind me of how decent the world is around us."

"And that's something else you need to hang on to," she added, with a big smile. "And again, don't go down the pathway of complete negativity, not until we know what the actual result of all this will be."

"I'll stay positive," he told her, "at least until then."

"Promise?" she asked, one eyebrow lifted. "I mean, a real promise. You can't let this derail you. You'll work hard to get yourself back on track, as much as you can, for yourself and for Timothy."

He nodded. "I promise."

"In that case, why don't we go for a long walk around and then maybe head back to the pool?"

"I can do that. I haven't been in the pool since we found out."

"Then today's a good day to switch that around," she murmured, "because it's a perfect day for a swim."

And that's what they did. She led him back to the main part of the center.

They parted ways, as she headed for her place to get changed. When she got back to the pool, she saw no sign of Spencer. She waited fretfully, until he suddenly showed up, with a smile on his face. "Hey, I'm glad you weren't any longer. I was about to come looking for you."

"Oh, not again," he said, with an eye roll. "That one fall

was bad enough."

"Hey, it wasn't so bad for you maybe, but it was bad for me," she muttered. "Particularly thinking that I should have gone looking for you earlier."

"Not at all."

And then she realized the difference in that big smile on his face. "What's the matter? Or maybe what's good?"

"Timothy gets to stay," he declared. "The VA, on Dani's appeal, have agreed to let Timothy stay for four months."

"Oh my gosh," she squealed, almost dancing on the spot. "That's perfect."

"Yeah. I know he's feeling a whole lot better about it now too. It's such a big relief."

"Good. Remember that part about miracles."

He looked up at her, and something fierce filled his expression. He motioned with his finger, crooking his hand to have her walk closer.

As she approached, she asked, "What's the matter?"

"Nothing's the matter. It's more a case of what's right."

She looked at him and asked, "And what is right?"

"You're right about miracles," he murmured. "You're a miracle. You're my miracle. I didn't even realize just how badly I was reacting to Timothy's status, and I couldn't change it, which just brought back tenfold all that sense of helplessness about his situation and about all the things that we've been through. Only in therapy could I put it all away. Only because of you pointing it out for me."

"Anybody could have done that for you," she said lightly.

"Maybe. Maybe anybody could have, but not everybody did. *You* did," Spencer declared, "and I mean it when I say you're a miracle. You're my miracle." And he locked his wheelchair and stood up very slowly on his good leg, and he opened his arms. She stepped into them, and he held her close. "And I promise. I'm not going anywhere, not now, not ever. The farthest I'll go is to town, and that's only until we can figure out how to make a life between us work."

She looked up in joy, feeling tears at his words pluck at the corners of her eyes. "Now that," she whispered, "sounds perfect." He tilted her chin, until her lips were pointed toward him, and he lowered his head and kissed her gently. "I mean it. I don't want this feeling to ever disappear."

"Neither do I," she whispered against his lips. "It's just way too special."

"And it's just about us, something that I never thought to have again." His arms crushed her close, and he whispered, "Please tell me that you feel the same way as I do."

"Oh, I do," she said, beaming up at him. "I absolutely feel the same way. I was just so afraid that you didn't. That's why I was skirting around the issue to see how you felt, to see what you were thinking," she admitted, with tears in her eyes.

"No more skirting around, no more wondering how I feel," he began, with a grin. "This is how I feel. You are not only a very special person but you've made a home in my heart." He paused. "If you ever walk away, I will be bereft," he murmured.

"I wasn't planning on it. Personally I think this relationship has permanent written all over it."

"The hole in my heart is filled too. So let's make it permanent," he said, crushing her against him, whispering into her ear. "Just know that I love you, and, wherever the future takes us, up or down or sideways, I just want you there at my side."

She wrapped her arms around his neck, as he held her closer, and she whispered, "Absolutely. That's all I ever wanted. Just you and me together. The two of us," she murmured. "I love you. Forever."

He looked down, murmured against her lips, and whispered, "Forever." And kissed her gently.

Epilogue

TIMOTHY STARED AT Dani, hating the burning sensation in his eyes, but also afraid to believe what she'd just told him, in case it wasn't true. "Are you serious?" he asked, as he crashed on his bed. "I can stay?"

She grinned at him. "We got four months out of them."

"Oh my God." He felt such a relief and a weight fall off his chest, which he'd never expected. When he looked up, a doctor stood in his doorway, the same doctor who he'd met many times since. "Dr. Savannah. Apparently it's official. I get to stay."

She looked over at Dani, and the two women smiled at each other. "Yep, you sure do," Dani confirmed.

"Now," Savannah said, rubbing her hands together, "I get to work you to the bone."

"Ha, I'm worried to the bone now," he murmured. "I've already been rode hard and put up wet."

"You have been," she agreed cheerfully, "and now that you know what rehab is here at Hathaway House, you should have no problem facing it."

At that, he got a little more worried. "The next workouts will be rougher, won't they?"

"I've got a meeting with Shane next," she shared. "Four months is a decent amount of time. I would have preferred six. But"—she looked over at Dani—"we'll do the best we can. And that means you'll work your buns off."

"And that's okay," he stated. "I know what a gift it is to stay, and I fully expect to work as hard as I can to make good use of it." He looked over at Dani. "Thank you again."

She smiled. "There'll be paperwork though. There's always paperwork."

He groaned and nodded. "And that's fine. I'm happy to do whatever I need to do."

And, with that, Dani smiled and waved and disappeared.

The doctor looked at him and added, "Now maybe you'll relax."

"Now I can." He nodded. "Never even occurred to me that this scenario could happen. When it first hit me out of the blue, I admit I didn't handle it well."

"You've been given a huge gift," she said. "Now we just have to put it to good use."

"Oh, I will," he declared fervently. "I will."

She smiled at him. "In that case, we'll see you tomorrow morning."

"Wait. So I'll see you and Shane about my revised rehab program?"

She nodded. "I've been picking up some new techniques," she shared. "I want to run you through some more tests, see if we can amplify some of your progress."

"Sounds good," Timothy replied. She just smiled and disappeared. He relaxed on his bed, and—alone for the first time since hearing the good news—he let the hot tears leak from the corners of his eyes, before he wiped them away impatiently.

"You idiot, no point in crying," he murmured. "It's all good. Now to make the best use you can of being here because you never know when this will happen again. So, promise yourself you'll do this, and you'll do this well. No more bellyaching, no more whining, no nothing. Just progress and then get your butt out of here," he murmured.

And, with that pep talk done, he sent a quick text to Spencer.

Then Timothy fell asleep with a huge smile on his face.

This concludes Book 19 of Hathaway House: Spencer.
Read about Timothy: Hathaway House, Book 20

Hathaway House: Timothy (Book #20)

Welcome to Hathaway House. Rehab Center. Safe Haven. Second chance at life and love.

With funding problems a nagging issue and completely overshadowing his stay at Hathaway House, Timothy finds it hard to do anything but drive himself forward as fast and as hard as he can—even against doctor's orders. But he wants to make the most of his time here, and knowing his stay could be rescinded at any moment is an added stress he doesn't need.

Savannah became a doctor to help people. Her parents were delighted, until she decided that Hathaway House suited her perfectly. Her parents felt she'd shortchanged herself, had taken an easy career instead of a prestigious one—that she wasn't driven enough to make a success of her life. Maybe they were right, but she was happy, and surely that should count for something.

Seeing Timothy push himself to the extreme, as she gently tries to help him destress, brings up fears on both sides and also a need to help each other find that so-necessary balance in life—and maybe, with luck, find each other.

Find Book 20 here!
To find out more visit Dale Mayer's website.
https://geni.us/DMSTimothy

Author's Note

Thank you for reading Spencer: Hathaway House, Book 19! If you enjoyed the book, please take a moment and leave a short review.

Dear reader,

I love to hear from readers, and you can contact me at my website: www.dalemayer.com or at my Facebook author page. To be informed of new releases and special offers, sign up for my newsletter or follow me on BookBub. And if you are interested in joining Dale Mayer's Reader Group, here is the Facebook sign up page.
http://geni.us/DaleMayerFBGroup

Cheers,
Dale Mayer

About the Author

Dale Mayer is a *USA Today* best-selling author, best known for her SEALs military romances, her Psychic Visions series, and her Lovely Lethal Garden cozy series. Her contemporary romances are raw and full of passion and emotion (Broken But … Mending, Hathaway House series). Her thrillers will keep you guessing (Kate Morgan, By Death series), and her romantic comedies will keep you giggling (*It's a Dog's Life*, a stand-alone novella; and the Broken Protocols series, starring Charming Marvin, the cat).

Dale honors the stories that come to her—and some of them are crazy, break all the rules and cross multiple genres!

To go with her fiction, she also writes nonfiction in many different fields, with books available on résumé writing, companion gardening, and the US mortgage system. All her books are available in print and ebook format.

Connect with Dale Mayer Online

Dale's Website – www.dalemayer.com
Twitter – @DaleMayer
Facebook Page – geni.us/DaleMayerFBFanPage
Facebook Group – geni.us/DaleMayerFBGroup
BookBub – geni.us/DaleMayerBookbub
Instagram – geni.us/DaleMayerInstagram
Goodreads – geni.us/DaleMayerGoodreads
Newsletter – geni.us/DaleNews

Also by Dale Mayer

Published Adult Books:

Shadow Recon
Magnus, Book 1
Rogan, Book 2

Bullard's Battle
Ryland's Reach, Book 1
Cain's Cross, Book 2
Eton's Escape, Book 3
Garret's Gambit, Book 4
Kano's Keep, Book 5
Fallon's Flaw, Book 6
Quinn's Quest, Book 7
Bullard's Beauty, Book 8
Bullard's Best, Book 9
Bullard's Battle, Books 1–2
Bullard's Battle, Books 3–4
Bullard's Battle, Books 5–6
Bullard's Battle, Books 7–8

Terkel's Team
Damon's Deal, Book 1
Wade's War, Book 2
Gage's Goal, Book 3
Calum's Contact, Book 4
Rick's Road, Book 5

Scott's Summit, Book 6
Brody's Beast, Book 7
Terkel's Twist, Book 8
Terkel's Triumph, Book 9

Terkel's Guardian
Radar, Book 1

Kate Morgan
Simon Says… Hide, Book 1
Simon Says… Jump, Book 2
Simon Says… Ride, Book 3
Simon Says… Scream, Book 4
Simon Says… Run, Book 5
Simon Says… Walk, Book 6

Hathaway House
Aaron, Book 1
Brock, Book 2
Cole, Book 3
Denton, Book 4
Elliot, Book 5
Finn, Book 6
Gregory, Book 7
Heath, Book 8
Iain, Book 9
Jaden, Book 10
Keith, Book 11
Lance, Book 12
Melissa, Book 13
Nash, Book 14
Owen, Book 15
Percy, Book 16

Quinton, Book 17
Ryatt, Book 18
Spencer, Book 19
Timothy, Book 20
Hathaway House, Books 1–3
Hathaway House, Books 4–6
Hathaway House, Books 7–9

The K9 Files
Ethan, Book 1
Pierce, Book 2
Zane, Book 3
Blaze, Book 4
Lucas, Book 5
Parker, Book 6
Carter, Book 7
Weston, Book 8
Greyson, Book 9
Rowan, Book 10
Caleb, Book 11
Kurt, Book 12
Tucker, Book 13
Harley, Book 14
Kyron, Book 15
Jenner, Book 16
Rhys, Book 17
Landon, Book 18
Harper, Book 19
Kascius, Book 20
The K9 Files, Books 1–2
The K9 Files, Books 3–4
The K9 Files, Books 5–6

The K9 Files, Books 7–8
The K9 Files, Books 9–10
The K9 Files, Books 11–12

Lovely Lethal Gardens
Arsenic in the Azaleas, Book 1
Bones in the Begonias, Book 2
Corpse in the Carnations, Book 3
Daggers in the Dahlias, Book 4
Evidence in the Echinacea, Book 5
Footprints in the Ferns, Book 6
Gun in the Gardenias, Book 7
Handcuffs in the Heather, Book 8
Ice Pick in the Ivy, Book 9
Jewels in the Juniper, Book 10
Killer in the Kiwis, Book 11
Lifeless in the Lilies, Book 12
Murder in the Marigolds, Book 13
Nabbed in the Nasturtiums, Book 14
Offed in the Orchids, Book 15
Poison in the Pansies, Book 16
Quarry in the Quince, Book 17
Revenge in the Roses, Book 18
Silenced in the Sunflowers, Book 19
Toes up in the Tulips, Book 20
Uzi in the Urn, Book 21
Lovely Lethal Gardens, Books 1–2
Lovely Lethal Gardens, Books 3–4
Lovely Lethal Gardens, Books 5–6
Lovely Lethal Gardens, Books 7–8
Lovely Lethal Gardens, Books 9–10

Psychic Visions Series
Tuesday's Child
Hide 'n Go Seek
Maddy's Floor
Garden of Sorrow
Knock Knock…
Rare Find
Eyes to the Soul
Now You See Her
Shattered
Into the Abyss
Seeds of Malice
Eye of the Falcon
Itsy-Bitsy Spider
Unmasked
Deep Beneath
From the Ashes
Stroke of Death
Ice Maiden
Snap, Crackle…
What If…
Talking Bones
String of Tears
Inked Forever
Psychic Visions Books 1–3
Psychic Visions Books 4–6
Psychic Visions Books 7–9

By Death Series
Touched by Death
Haunted by Death
Chilled by Death

By Death Books 1–3

Broken Protocols – Romantic Comedy Series
Cat's Meow
Cat's Pajamas
Cat's Cradle
Cat's Claus
Broken Protocols 1-4

Broken and... Mending
Skin
Scars
Scales (of Justice)
Broken but... Mending 1-3

Glory
Genesis
Tori
Celeste
Glory Trilogy

Biker Blues
Morgan: Biker Blues, Volume 1
Cash: Biker Blues, Volume 2

SEALs of Honor
Mason: SEALs of Honor, Book 1
Hawk: SEALs of Honor, Book 2
Dane: SEALs of Honor, Book 3
Swede: SEALs of Honor, Book 4
Shadow: SEALs of Honor, Book 5
Cooper: SEALs of Honor, Book 6
Markus: SEALs of Honor, Book 7

Evan: SEALs of Honor, Book 8
Mason's Wish: SEALs of Honor, Book 9
Chase: SEALs of Honor, Book 10
Brett: SEALs of Honor, Book 11
Devlin: SEALs of Honor, Book 12
Easton: SEALs of Honor, Book 13
Ryder: SEALs of Honor, Book 14
Macklin: SEALs of Honor, Book 15
Corey: SEALs of Honor, Book 16
Warrick: SEALs of Honor, Book 17
Tanner: SEALs of Honor, Book 18
Jackson: SEALs of Honor, Book 19
Kanen: SEALs of Honor, Book 20
Nelson: SEALs of Honor, Book 21
Taylor: SEALs of Honor, Book 22
Colton: SEALs of Honor, Book 23
Troy: SEALs of Honor, Book 24
Axel: SEALs of Honor, Book 25
Baylor: SEALs of Honor, Book 26
Hudson: SEALs of Honor, Book 27
Lachlan: SEALs of Honor, Book 28
Paxton: SEALs of Honor, Book 29
Bronson: SEALs of Honor, Book 30
Hale: SEALs of Honor, Book 31
SEALs of Honor, Books 1–3
SEALs of Honor, Books 4–6
SEALs of Honor, Books 7–10
SEALs of Honor, Books 11–13
SEALs of Honor, Books 14–16
SEALs of Honor, Books 17–19
SEALs of Honor, Books 20–22
SEALs of Honor, Books 23–25

Heroes for Hire
Levi's Legend: Heroes for Hire, Book 1
Stone's Surrender: Heroes for Hire, Book 2
Merk's Mistake: Heroes for Hire, Book 3
Rhodes's Reward: Heroes for Hire, Book 4
Flynn's Firecracker: Heroes for Hire, Book 5
Logan's Light: Heroes for Hire, Book 6
Harrison's Heart: Heroes for Hire, Book 7
Saul's Sweetheart: Heroes for Hire, Book 8
Dakota's Delight: Heroes for Hire, Book 9
Tyson's Treasure: Heroes for Hire, Book 10
Jace's Jewel: Heroes for Hire, Book 11
Rory's Rose: Heroes for Hire, Book 12
Brandon's Bliss: Heroes for Hire, Book 13
Liam's Lily: Heroes for Hire, Book 14
North's Nikki: Heroes for Hire, Book 15
Anders's Angel: Heroes for Hire, Book 16
Reyes's Raina: Heroes for Hire, Book 17
Dezi's Diamond: Heroes for Hire, Book 18
Vince's Vixen: Heroes for Hire, Book 19
Ice's Icing: Heroes for Hire, Book 20
Johan's Joy: Heroes for Hire, Book 21
Galen's Gemma: Heroes for Hire, Book 22
Zack's Zest: Heroes for Hire, Book 23
Bonaparte's Belle: Heroes for Hire, Book 24
Noah's Nemesis: Heroes for Hire, Book 25
Tomas's Trials: Heroes for Hire, Book 26
Carson's Choice: Heroes for Hire, Book 27
Dante's Decision: Heroes for Hire, Book 28
Steve's Solace: Heroes for Hire, Book 29
Heroes for Hire, Books 1–3
Heroes for Hire, Books 4–6

Heroes for Hire, Books 7–9
Heroes for Hire, Books 10–12
Heroes for Hire, Books 13–15
Heroes for Hire, Books 16–18
Heroes for Hire, Books 19–21
Heroes for Hire, Books 22–24

SEALs of Steel
Badger: SEALs of Steel, Book 1
Erick: SEALs of Steel, Book 2
Cade: SEALs of Steel, Book 3
Talon: SEALs of Steel, Book 4
Laszlo: SEALs of Steel, Book 5
Geir: SEALs of Steel, Book 6
Jager: SEALs of Steel, Book 7
The Final Reveal: SEALs of Steel, Book 8
SEALs of Steel, Books 1–4
SEALs of Steel, Books 5–8
SEALs of Steel, Books 1–8

The Mavericks
Kerrick, Book 1
Griffin, Book 2
Jax, Book 3
Beau, Book 4
Asher, Book 5
Ryker, Book 6
Miles, Book 7
Nico, Book 8
Keane, Book 9
Lennox, Book 10
Gavin, Book 11
Shane, Book 12

Diesel, Book 13
Jerricho, Book 14
Killian, Book 15
Hatch, Book 16
Corbin, Book 17
Aiden, Book 18
The Mavericks, Books 1–2
The Mavericks, Books 3–4
The Mavericks, Books 5–6
The Mavericks, Books 7–8
The Mavericks, Books 9–10
The Mavericks, Books 11–12

Standalone Novellas
It's a Dog's Life
Riana's Revenge
Second Chances

Published Young Adult Books:

Family Blood Ties Series
Vampire in Denial
Vampire in Distress
Vampire in Design
Vampire in Deceit
Vampire in Defiance
Vampire in Conflict
Vampire in Chaos
Vampire in Crisis
Vampire in Control
Vampire in Charge
Family Blood Ties Set 1–3
Family Blood Ties Set 1–5

Family Blood Ties Set 4–6
Family Blood Ties Set 7–9
Sian's Solution, A Family Blood Ties Series Prequel Novelette

Design series
Dangerous Designs
Deadly Designs
Darkest Designs
Design Series Trilogy

Standalone
In Cassie's Corner
Gem Stone (a Gemma Stone Mystery)
Time Thieves

Published Non-Fiction Books:

Career Essentials
Career Essentials: The Résumé
Career Essentials: The Cover Letter
Career Essentials: The Interview
Career Essentials: 3 in 1